Retirement
A slave's voyage of self-discovery

Part III of a Trilogy

Christopher Charlton

EmOhErotica
Leeds, UK

i

Published by EmOh Erotica, PO Box HP346, Leeds LS6 1UL, UK

British Library Cataloguing-in-Publication data: Chris Charlton

Retirement; a slave's voyage of self-discovery – Part III of a Trilogy,

1. Title

ISBN   978-1-873031-41-2 (Kindle)
        978-1-873031-43-8 (Paperback)

Cover design: Ben Matthews

FOR

Mr McC and raz

ALSO BY CHRISTOPHER CHARLTON

Revelation –
Part I of a Slave's Voyage of Self-Discovery

Rennaisance –
Part II of a Slave's Voyage of Self-Discovery

The Key to Life:
How to Get More Out of Chastity for Men

CONTENTS

Acknowledgements

I had been trying unsuccessfully to reconcile Old Guard attitudes with changing beliefs when I met Ward. We talked. He challenged me and provided me with direction. I thank him for the conversation that gave me some answers, showed me the way to find others and instilled in me the inspiration which later prompted this story.

CC

Meeting Andrew

How the hell did he get like that? I closed my eyes and looked again, in case I really couldn't believe what I was seeing.

The man was muscled in a way that a twenty-year-old would be. He was lithe, defined, slim, fit, but there was no way he was that young; he had to be at least thirty, perhaps even forty years older than that. I watched as he went on his way across the run site. He was following a taller, definitely older, man – a leash linking a gloved hand to a studded black leather collar around the fitter man's neck. I stood open-mouthed as the pair crossed the compound. The Master was at least six three, I thought, slim, his gray hair closely- cropped. He was dressed from neck to toe in immaculate black leather. He seemed familiar but, try as I could, I failed to put a name to the face.

The Adonis behind him had all my attention. He was probably a foot shorter than his Master, but was dressed only in tight leather shorts, a heavy padlocked chain accompanying the collar around his neck, and black work boots, with an inch or so of white sock visible around each of his lower legs.

Just as intriguingly, the smaller man was gagged and handcuffed. He was trying to balance himself as he crossed the uneven ground with his hands in front of him carrying what looked like a doctor's bag.

I wanted to get closer, but they were both moving quickly. I had no chance of getting passed the whippings and floggings on the various crosses between me and them before they disappeared into the woods around the run site.

I stood there, silent, motionless. I was starting to get hard. I was jealous. I wanted to have a body like that and be on a chain like that. My emotions must have been truly obvious.

No more than a few seconds had passed before Eli, an old friend, slapped me on the back.

'They are amazing, aren't they?' he said.

'Sure.' It was all I could say. I was still mesmerized. 'Or rather he's amazing.'

I snapped out of my daze.

'The smaller guy? Definitely. Hot, hot, hot, hot, hot,' I said, my mouth hanging open. Eli couldn't have failed to notice the target of my attention.

'They're quite something.' I turned to face Eli.

'You know them?' I demanded. 'Sure. Everyone knows them.'

'Introduce me then.'

'Well.' Eli was backtracking. 'I know who they are. I've seen them around, but I don't know them to talk to.'

I was disappointed.

'OK, wise guy,' I said, sarcastically, 'who are they then?'

'I'm surprised you don't know.' It was Eli's turn to tease me.

'No,' I said, 'I don't.'

Eli waited. I was about to hit him when he finally spoke.

'The Master, he's a Brit, a top businessman, ran an investment bank before he retired, he's quite someone, that's Lord Amos Cunningham.'

Of course, I thought. He was a familiar figure on the pages of the *Financial Times* and the TV business shows.

I pushed such thoughts out of my mind; I'd come back to them later.

'Who's the guy with him?'

Eli turned and looked at me, baiting me, keeping me waiting again. I was impatient to know the identity of the man who, a few seconds earlier, had made such a mark on my retinas.

'Oh,' said Eli, 'that's Andrew.'

'Andrew?'

'Yeh. Everyone just knows him as Andrew.'

'I haven't seen them before,' I said.

'They've been around,' responded Eli, 'but, now you mention it, not for a while.'

I pursed my mouth, thinking.

'Are you happy now?' Eli asked.

I nodded.

'Be careful,' he added. 'Lord Amos is heavy.'

I was just about to start telling Eli in my 'correct British way' that it was Lord Cunningham or, as he'd been at one time, Sir Amos Cunningham, when he slapped me amicably across the shoulders and walked away.

I stood there a while longer.

I ignored the scenes taking place around me. I was deaf to the sounds of leather floggers and single-tail whips hitting the flesh of men's backs. I ignored the naked men in cages, those in body bags hanging from wooden scaffolds, the guy on all-fours playing at being a dog, lifting his leg to piss against a plastic fire hydrant.

All I wanted at that moment was to meet Andrew, and talk to him. I knew I'd have to be patient, perhaps approach his Master, the renowned Lord Cunningham, at dinner, to ask permission.

I sighed. I'd find play distracting until I knew more. I turned and made my way towards the pool. The best way, I thought, was to try to relax during the few hours before dinner, rather than get too neurotic. I had got to know myself quite well over the years. Introspection has a few advantages. Fixations had been the bane of my life. Andrew, I realized, had – unknowingly to him – become the latest.

Despite trying to calm down, my mind ran riot that

afternoon. The Ohio sun was pleasantly warm, the temperature was in the low eighties and there was little or no humidity. It was weather I liked. It was nicely comfortable. I smiled as I watched men being boys as they frolicked in the pool, showing off amazing tattoos and their private piercings as they threw off their shorts and their inhibitions to take advantage of the nakedness that was allowed once the run had started. Even the larger guys had something attractive about them, relaxed like that, I thought, but my mind was more interested in Andrew. The questions were lining themselves up. Who was he? Where had he come from? How had he got himself into such amazing shape? How had he met someone as influential, so close to politicians, governments and power, as Lord Cunningham? How could I get a job like that too? I wanted answers, but I also knew I had to wait if I was to stand any chance of getting them.

* * *

I was among the first in line for cocktails before dinner that evening. I was determined to get to Lord Cunningham as soon as he arrived, to ask for his permission to talk to Andrew. I'd gone back to the cabin where I was staying, showered and shaved for the second time that day. Normally at runs, I would be scruffier than usual. I always carried more clothes and more baggage across the Atlantic with me than I ever used. This particular evening, I'd pulled a clean shirt from my bag. I wanted to be smart for His Lordship.

I was excited to meet Andrew, so anxious that I'd even forgotten to remind the bartenders that I only wanted a 'British amount' of ice with my gin-and-tonics. I think I was on my third generous measure when His Lordship at last appeared. Andrew was on a leash, a few steps behind him. They looked good.

The deck around the bar was busy, most of the two hundred guys on the run were there. Getting to the hot pair took me a few minutes. I was lucky as I approached.

'Hey, Russ,' I heard as I made my way through the crowd. 'Come and meet another Brit.'

I wasn't given much choice. I had been so concentrating on Andrew that I hadn't seen another old friend. I felt that my prayers had been answered when Larry Trenton grabbed me. I just had time to hold out my hand.

Amos, Lord Cunningham, had changed into an immaculate uniform, even though the run's formal dinner didn't take place until the following evening. I'd forgotten that before going into industry and becoming CEO of one of the UK's top investment companies, he'd been in the Royal Navy, rising to the rank of Commodore by the time he was in his early thirties. He'd gone on to become a Rear Admiral in the reserve. Amos Cunningham had been a high flyer from the moment he'd been born.

But this Amos Cunningham was a side of the man that few got to see. I'd heard rumors of course, everyone in the UK had. His sexuality was one of the most open secrets in the City of London. One or two of the men I knew there, business leaders themselves, had speculated about deeper interests, but Cunningham had been careful, discrete. He'd managed to keep himself out of the public eye.

'Amos, meet Russ,' Larry said. 'Russ, meet Amos.'

'Your Lordship,' I said, looking up into the tall man's eyes as I shook his hand. He had the grace to laugh.

'Russ,' he said. 'A pleasure. It's good to find someone who appreciates the terminology.'

I nodded. Aristocrats from the UK were perpetually

frustrated by Americans' apparent inability to tell their majesties from their highnesses, their peers from their piers, and their knights from their days.

'I understand, Sir,' I said, wondering how some of those around me would cope with addressing episcopalian bishops as 'Your Grace.' Using 'Sir' was both acceptable to the protocol of the House of Lords in Westminster, London, and to the rarer, alternative culture of leather runs.

'Yes,' he said. 'Being Lord Amos or Sir Cunningham gets a tiresome after a while.'

Larry looked on. He'd worked in government affairs in London. He understood. That's how we'd met. It was, I guessed, probably how he'd met Amos, Lord Cunningham too.

Despite his rank, Lord Cunningham joined the line for the bar. Larry stayed with him. He'd shaken my hand with his right, keeping Andrew's leash in his left, I noticed. I saw that the smaller man was now wearing tight white shorts and a bar vest. Unlike the club colors adorning many of the black leather vests around us, Andrew's carried the armorial crest of Amos, Lord Cunningham of Huby in the county of North Yorkshire. Even if others there didn't appreciate the significance, I liked the style.

As they neared being served, His Lordship dropped Andrew's leash. We talked more as we waited, about the weather, mutual friends, concentrating on the niceties of social small-talk. Curious as I was about Amos Cunningham as a businessman and, now, a politician, my nice, white, middle-class, Anglo-Saxon conditioning told me that I should get to know His Lordship more before being so forward with such questions. I'd been to boarding school, I thought. I could do deference. And, I remembered, if the Financial Times was to be believed, Amos Cunningham was renowned for his ego as well as his wealth.

Apart from which, I was curious about Andrew. I grinned as I saw that the line for cocktails had come to a stop while he taught the volunteer bartenders how to fix a pink gin.

Andrew bowed as he held out the drinks for his Master and Larry. Amos Cunningham said nothing, but nodded an acknowledgement. Andrew returned to the line. I watched him out of the corner of my eye, as he got a drink for himself.

Having joined this select group, I had no intention of being squeezed out of it.

I listened patiently as Lord Cunningham answered more inevitable questions about the House of Saxe-Gotha-Coburg-Battenburg- Windsor and its relationships – constitutional, political and familial. I think I won Amos Cunningham's approval and acceptance when I stepped in to rescue him. I hadn't really appreciated the classes during my last years at school on the UK monarchy and constitution until I started visiting the USA. He seemed relieved when I rehearsed, yet again, anecdotes about Diana, Princess of Wales, and Queen Elizabeth, the Queen Mother.

I asked the question when His Lordship leaned forward to thank me for the intervention.

I got the reply I had been hoping for.

'Of course,' he said, smiling, 'but just don't get in Andrew's way. He is here to work, you know.'

I watched Andrew and Amos Cunningham as closely as I could without appearing too nosy when I sat with them at dinner.

Away from the crowd at the bar, I could see that every crease of the Master's uniform was sharp and in its place. The peak of his cap shone like a mirror. His boots did too. Andrew should be proud of his work, I felt.

I looked more closely at the shorts. They were brief, just

covering the cheeks of his ass, and almost see-through in a white that matched the Master's uniform shirt. I noticed too the navy blue trim.

Despite the cuffs around his wrists, Andrew had fetched his Master's meal. He'd was allowed to eat too, but had to do so kneeling on the ground beside the Master's chair.

Sitting so close to Andrew, I could see that there didn't seem to be a spare ounce of body fat on him. His pecs were beautifully defined, his abdominal muscles clear too. His butt was pert and there was no evidence of the 'spread' that hits the hips of so many men in middle age. I caught my mouth dropping open at the thought of licking his well-formed thighs and his firm flesh. Apart from his eyebrows, there did not seem to be a single hair on his body. A chain ran between metal bands locked around his ankles. I thought I could see bindings on his cock and balls inside the tight white shorts.

After dinner, Andrew fetched His Lordship another drink; brandy, I think. Andrew knelt to as he presented the glass to his Master, a sight that was truly beautiful, but also exceedingly distracting. I had to concentrate hard to maintain my side of conversation. Larry and His Lordship had moved onto UK-US politics, looking to me for a journalist's perspective whenever they thought it necessary. I was getting impatient. I wanted my private time with Andrew to begin. I thought my mind had been going crazy about him that afternoon.

If anything, the proximity was making my infatuation more intense. Andrew was so hot. I felt so, so, so ashamed. There was this man, at least twenty years older than me, in such good shape. I had seen men over fifty who entered the veterans' classes in bodybuilding competitions. This guy was different. It wasn't that sort of heavily-built muscle.

Andrew wasn't tall. I'm five foot six and he was shorter than me. The muscle was defined without being bulky, that was it.

And there was nothing, and I mean nothing, on his hips. I felt so envious.

I'd teased myself about having a thirty-inch waist for my thirtieth birthday. I hadn't been far off, but I'd put on weight and lost it and put it on again after that. I'd thought, that summer, that I wouldn't lose weight again. I'd finally given all my smaller clothes to a thrift store. Then, I'd seen Andrew. Now I was waiting to talk to him.

Andrew had been kneeling, saying nothing. It wasn't until he noticed my watch that he brought a finger to his lips.

He had to wait a few moments before Amos Cunningham noticed. 'Yes, Andrew?' he said.

'If Master wishes, Sir, there is work to be done.'

Andrew's words were quiet but entirely submissive. I was even more impressed than when I'd first seen him.

Lord Cunningham reached for my wrist.

'Yes,' he said, looking at my watch, 'that's a good idea. Russ, go with him, you can talk as he works.'

I stood and bowed; words didn't seem necessary.

'But do come back and join us when he's finished. I'd like that.'

I nodded again. I was honored.

His Lordship pulled a key from his pocket and unlocked the restraints from Andrew's wrists.

It wasn't until we were out of his Master's hearing, leaving the dining area, that Andrew spoke.

'I have about an hour, Sir,' he said to me, 'then I have to be ready to assist the Master with a scene at midnight.'

I nodded. I was just pleased to have any time I could with him.

I watched as he moved. Even in the darkness of the evening, I could see the sinews in his body as he walked. I noticed the restraints on his wrists and ankles. They were heavy steel. Each must have weighed several pounds. No wonder he was in such good shape.

The metal links of the chain around his neck were about half an inch in diameter. I hated to think of the pressure it was putting on Andrew's chest.

When we got to the Master's cabin, Andrew stopped. There, on the porch, was a line of boots.

'As he said, we can talk while I work,' said Andrew as he reached into a box for polish, brushes and cloths.

'That's fine,' I answered. I had no wish whatsoever to get between this exemplar slave and his Master's requirements.

* * *

Andrew was nothing if not generous. Having been given permission to talk to me, and answer my questions, he was exceedingly fulsome. He spoke for around an hour that evening. I sat on a chair listening, prompting. Andrew sat cross-legged on the floor. He'd taken off the vest and white shorts so they didn't get marked as he polished his Master's boots. I saw the clear plastic chastity device locked around his cock and balls for the first time. I looked at him enviously.

Andrew told me that he had retired early. He had been a professor at one of the state universities. He'd been married, but his wife had died just after he'd finished work. He'd had the chance to stop when he was fifty-five. During more than thirty years at the university, he had built up an ample retirement fund. Private tuition fees had helped too, he said.

Andrew told me about his wife. As he became more

comfortable talking to me, he revealed more. They'd been close all through school, and, with the blessings of both her parents and his, they'd married when they were both eighteen. They'd worked their way through college. They both went to graduate school, then he got a post at a university in the neighboring state, primarily teaching but also doing some research. They were in their twenties when they became parents to a son, George, a daughter, Annie. I have grandchildren now too, he added. Andrew told me that he thought it was when he was nearly thirty, after their children were born, that he started to appreciate that he may not really have been heterosexual, and that he had other needs, but he loved Mary, his wife, so much, that he hadn't thought much about it. He said that they stopped having sex then, but they were very, very close, companions, sharing many aspects of their lives. He enjoyed teaching. He wasn't ambitious but loved encouraging and nurturing his students. I bet he was a wonderful tutor. She went into pastoral work, helping out on the campus. It seems they were modest, but very happy.

When the chance came, I learned, Andrew and Mary decided he should retire. They could live economically and travel some. They would get an RV and drive from coast to coast, from Canada to Mexico, Alaska to Key West; they drew up a five-year plan. When they were sixty, they decided they would go further afield, perhaps trying a different continent each year. Exploring Europe would be just the start. The circle of Australia would follow.

They'd not long started their first domestic US trip when tragedy hit. They'd driven to Seattle and then south as close to the coast as they could to get to San Francisco. There, they spent some time with their daughter. They were heading along the Pacific Coast Highway after that, heading further south, Andrew told me, when Mary had a blackout. He rushed her to a local hospital, but they had her airlifted to LA. When he got there, very early the next morning, he was told the news: Mary had a huge, inoperable tumor. The hospital offered her radiotherapy and chemo, but she said no. She'd always been fit, well and healthy, and, Andrew told me, she couldn't face being ill.

I hadn't expected all this when I'd started talking to him, but it was what he told me. There was still pain; it was in his eyes as he spoke, but while there were tears, there was no crying. Andrew continued his work, rubbing away, shining the boots as he told me more of his life story.

He said that, looking back, Mary had died as soon as she heard the diagnosis. At least, he said, her spirit had left her. He stayed with her in the hospital. It was, he said, very quick. She was only there three days.

She blacked out two or three times more he said, but she had become gray, her eyes sullen and sunken. She had held his hand. She wasn't scared, Andrew said she'd told him. She thanked him for the joy, their friendship, their partnership, the wonderful experiences they had shared. He called the children, Andrew said, but before they'd arrived, Mary had spoken to him long and hard. He was not old, she had said, he had time to find a new life. He was financially secure. He had a chance now to find himself, to discover the life that he wanted, and to live it. He was to enjoy the memories, to remember her and appreciate the good times, but he was not to let her passing destroy him. 'She held my hand, hard, and made me promise,' Andrew told me.

I was crying as Andrew told me more.

Mary had died in the hospital room. The children were with them. They'd had a party in the hospital. Mary had sent Andrew out to a store to buy champagne. They'd drunk a toast to life and to love. Then, in her own time and in her own way, she let go of life.

Andrew had driven her body home in its coffin in the back of the RV himself. There had been a funeral service at the university and a huge party there too. Mary's life had truly been celebrated. Andrew hadn't been sure what to do with Mary's ashes, but the university wanted to do something as a tribute. They planted a grove of trees and put the urn beside the roots. It felt right, he said. There's even a plaque there now, in her honor, he added.

When he'd got home, he'd found a letter from her. She'd written to him from her bed in the hospital and persuaded one of the nurses to mail the envelope. She had said again what she had to say, but she had also put in a single sheet; there were few words: 'Find yourself. Discover the life you want. Live the life you need.'

On the back of that sheet of paper, she'd written, lightly, in pencil: 'Frame this; look at it every day', Andrew said, so he had.

'I did what she wanted. I put it in the kitchen, near the fridge, so it was one of the first things I saw each day. I also had some copies made, he said. I keep one in my pocket book all the time' he added, smiling.

It took me a while to realize just how much she knew and how much permission she had given me, Andrew said. It took me a little while to tidy everything up, to sort out her affairs. She had been as neat and comprehensive in her will as she had been with anything in life, he said. All her clothes were left to Good Will stores; her books to the university library, her collection of local artefacts to the museum. Andrew had stopped at that point. I had had to prompt him. It was,

I said, quite a step from there to being someone's slave at a run. I hoped I'd spoken appropriately and the comment wasn't insensitive. I hadn't meant it to be. I was so full of admiration for this man and his love, but I was still unsure of the transformation. I wanted to know more, much more. I hoped he'd tell me.

'Where was I?' he asked, regaining his thoughts.

'The death of your wife,' I said, trying to be careful about any sensitivities.

'I remember,' he said.

'What happened then?' I asked.

'It was,' explained Andrew, 'a sequence of surprises.'

He paused, thinking, remembering. I remained silent, again letting him take up the story the way he wanted to tell it.

He started quietly.

I had a call from a former colleague in Philadelphia, Andrew said. He'd been out of the country, teaching in Europe. He'd arrived home to find a letter telling him about Mary's sudden death. He'd expressed his sympathies, offered condolences. Then, he said, why not come visit? Have a change. A break for a few days. You can have the run of my home. As long as you want.

I had to say it seemed an excellent idea. I'd been thinking about getting away, having a vacation, but I'd no idea where I wanted to go. I wanted some space on my own, but I didn't want to be alone. A trip to the East Coast suited me too. Philadelphia was so convenient. If I felt like being a tourist, I could easily visit DC or New York. Yes, I said, before Donaldson – that's what this colleague of old was called – could hang up, I'll come.

I got there the next weekend. Donaldson met me at the airport. No one ever used Professor Donaldson's first name; he never used it. He signed everything, even academic papers, with his initials – LJ – but everyone called him Donaldson. I've never found out what the L and the J stand for. Donaldson had been more like a first name than a family name for years.

It was so good to see him. He was in good shape too. He looked well, fit, happy. I tried to recall when I'd last seen him. Although we'd met occasionally when his duties as an examiner had brought him out to the West Coast, I couldn't remember ever having visited his home. He put me right though. I had stayed with him, he reminded me, in New York, for one night several years before. He'd had a minuscule apartment in a co-op in Manhattan, not that far from the World Trade Center, where the Twins Towers used to stand. We'd had to share a bed, but we'd been drinking and hadn't thought anything of it. I knew Donaldson was gay, but he didn't flaunt it, certainly not when he was on campus or working. He was elegant, but not ostentatiously affluent. I remember him for his neatness. His shirts were always impeccably pressed, his pant creases precisely sharp.

He was waiting for me at the gate. He opened his arms and gave me a huge, warm, loving bear-hug. I hadn't wanted to cry until then. I put my arms around him and held him tightly. I didn't care about anyone else. I put my head against his chest. He wasn't huge, a little under six foot, but he was strong. His body felt firm. I wanted to hold him and weep. Donaldson let me stay there for a moment. He then held my hand. He didn't say anything. His eyes said it all. He could read my feelings. In one expression, he let me know that any words he could have chosen would have been weak and potentially meaningless. The look and the touch were far more real, genuine, lasting expressions of concern and support.

He'd taken my bag. It was summer and I hadn't packed

much. I was wearing jeans. I'd put some chinos, a couple of respectable shirts, shorts, swimwear, a couple of jockstraps and some socks in, that was all. He put his other arm around my shoulders.

'I am pleased to see you, Andrew,' Donaldson had said. 'You know you're more than welcome to stay as long as you like. I have some work to do, but make yourself at home.'

I felt honored. It was just the sort of escape that I needed, but I hadn't realized quite what an opening it would be.

Luke

Donaldson walked me out of the airport building and across to the parking lot, said Andrew, continuing his story. I let him continue in his own words.

We'd not got very far when a muscled young man arrived in front of us, wearing a tight-fitting yellow polo shirt and very tight buttock-length shorts.

Donaldson handed him my bag.

'Andrew,' he'd said, 'this is Luke.'

I'd nodded an acknowledgement.

'Pleased to meet you, Sir,' Luke had said.

Donaldson was still talking to me as Luke took up a position walking a pace or two behind us. He'd stayed at that distance for a few moments as we walked. When we were about fifteen yards from the car, Luke suddenly hurried ahead. By the time we'd reached the vehicle, my bag was in the trunk and the back doors were opened for us. Luke was waiting beside the left side door. As soon as Donaldson had got in, Luke shut the door. Within seconds, he was round the vehicle, beside me, closing my door too.

I had to try hard to take this interaction as nonchalantly as both Donaldson and the young man had done,' said Andrew.

The appearance of Luke had taken me a little unawares, but at the same time, Andrew continued. I knew that I was neither surprised nor shocked by either his presence there or his behavior. Even the short shorts weren't out of place on him. Somehow, it seemed entirely appropriate that Donaldson should have someone like that, doing what he was doing.

Donaldson and I talked as Luke drove us home. He expressed his sympathy again, expressing his regrets and commiserations about Mary. I pulled out my pocket book and showed him the photograph of the message she'd left me. His eyebrows rose with interest. I didn't appreciate the significance at the time.

I can't say that I remember the car stopping. I do remember Luke being so quick that he'd opened Donaldson's door for him to get out before I'd even realized we'd reached the house. Seconds later, before I could do it myself, he'd opened the door for me too. As soon as I was up and standing, he was gone.

By the time Donaldson had guided me towards the front door, it was being opened from the inside. Not only had Luke unlocked the back door and gone in, he'd had time to shed the shirt and shorts. I must admit I was greatly impressed by the muscle-toned young hunk now wearing only tight swim briefs holding the door open for us. The rings through each of his nipples shone in the bright late afternoon sunshine. I looked around as we went in. I could see my bag waiting at the bottom of the stairs. I had to admit that the young man was good.

Donaldson turned towards him.

'Show Professor Torrington to his room, Luke, so he can freshen up. Then bring me a drink. I'll be on the deck.'

'I'll see you in a moment, Andrew,' he said to me. 'Do excuse me while I make a few calls.'

Luke picked up my bag. It was clear that I should follow.

'Call me Andrew,' I said to him as soon as Donaldson was out of earshot, 'I'm retired now, I'm not really a professor any more.'

He turned before answering.

'I'll call you "Andrew, Sir", if I may?' he said.

Somehow, perhaps instinctively, I knew I should respect his request for the formality.

'You may. I would like that,' I said. 'Thank you.'

Luke showed me to my room. It was light and airy.

'If there's anything you need, Andrew Sir,' he said, 'you only have to call.

'The house is very private. No one can see in and the yard at the back is not overlooked. You don't have to wear clothes if you don't want to, Andrew Sir,' he added.

I nodded as I started to open my bag.

'I'll unpack for you,' said Luke. 'There are towels here, Andrew Sir,' he added, showing me the shower room.

'I change them every day and there are more down beside the pool. If you have any laundry, Andrew Sir, then just leave it here,' he said, indicating a wicker basket. Somehow I just knew that the service provided by Luke would be more caring and a higher quality than some of the most professional and expensive city laundries.

I sat on the bed.

No sooner had I lifted my leg and started to reach for my boots than Luke was there, kneeling, undoing them for me. It was strange. I had a feeling that I should have been embarrassed, or at least uncomfortable with such intimate service, but at the same time I could feel my cock starting to rise inside my own underwear. Within seconds, Luke had taken off my boots and placed them neatly to one side.

'Socks, Sir?' he inquired.

I nodded.

Again, swiftly and silently, he was there on his knees. Each sock was quickly removed, shaken discretely and taken to the laundry basket. It felt good to relax after the long flight.

'A shower, Andrew Sir?'

That would be a good idea. I nodded. Then I could get some sun, perhaps even a swim, but it would be good to wash away the perspiration and grime of the flight first.

I had hardly had time to nod before Luke had the shower running. By the time I had stood up and taken off my jeans and shirt, he was standing beside me with a towel. It seemed the most natural thing to be doing. My jeans were on the floor.

I started to move to pick them up.

Luke spoke again then.

'That's all right, Sir,' he said. 'I'll look after things.'

I went red then for the first time. I'd chosen some very brief white cotton bikini underwear for the flight. I could feel my cock starting to harden inside them again. I was embarrassed now, as Luke bent down beside me to pick up my jeans. I watched as he removed the belt, curled it and put it on a dresser before folding the denim, opening a closet and putting it neatly on a hanger.

The embarrassment didn't last long.

There was something, I couldn't then identify or describe it, about Luke which made everything he did seem so ordinary, everyday and normal that I knew I shouldn't be in the least uncomfortable. I had to admit too that he was a very good-looking man. He didn't seem in the least abashed by his own attire, the Speedos which emphasized rather than hid his own cock. I could see his ballsac too, outlined against the tight material, pushed forward beautifully, obscenely.

It seemed from the way he was behaving that this young man would be acting as my valet too, at least for the time-being. I knew that I had nothing to hide. I knew too that he could see most of me through my tight white briefs. It would not be long before he saw me entirely naked. He'd probably see my cock hard at some time or other. I had nothing to be ashamed of, I told myself.

I pushed my briefs down.

I was a little surprised then.

Before I had had time to bend and pick them up, Luke was on his knees. His hands were behind his back and his head was bent forward. I knew already that the last thing I should do was interfere. I stepped out of the briefs. Within a second, Luke had picked them up with his teeth and had put them on the bed.

I stood holding the towel half in front of me. It was little protection, my erection was full now.

'What will you be needing after your shower, Andrew Sir?' Luke asked.

I thought for a minute. I looked at the clock. It was early evening. I'd have time for a swim before dinner.

'Speedos,' I said, 'and then shorts and a tee-shirt for dinner.'

As I stepped into the shower, I saw Luke again pick up my briefs in his mouth and then carry them carefully to the laundry basket.

As I was soaping myself, I watched as he unpacked my bag. I tried not to make my attention too obvious as he laid out my own swim briefs on the bed and put a tee-shirt and shorts ready on one side for later. I was as hard as a rock, but somehow, I didn't feel I could touch my cock.

My erection had gone down a little when I stepped out of the shower. Luke had left the room then. I dried myself off and put on the light blue Speedos; they felt good. I can't remember quite when I'd noticed it, probably many, many years earlier when I'd been lecturing in Europe, but at some time, I had realized that men in Europe and America have different ways of wearing underwear and swimwear. In Europe, the styles are cut so the cock can point upwards, resting along the belly, or perhaps sideways. In America, men seem to point their cocks downwards, forcing their balls back between their legs. Once I'd discovered the European way, there had been no alternative for me. Okay, the bulge could look far more prominent at times, but it seemed preferable and more comfortable than the American way. I preferred having my balls pushed forward. American men seemed set on showing that they had been circumcised. Luke, I suddenly noticed, had been wearing his swim briefs the European way.

I picked up a towel and went downstairs.

I crossed Donaldson's large open-plan living area towards the deck and the pool. I could see Luke, kneeling, handing him a wine glass. There was a bottle of Chardonnay on a nearby table. I couldn't see Donaldson's face; he was looking out across the pool. It wasn't until I got closer that I could see that he too had shed his street attire. He was wearing only some tight square-cut shorts. It was probably the first time in more than twenty years that I had seen him without a shirt. I had to admit to myself that he too looked very good. His chest was very well defined, even under his heavy pelt. The hair was graying in places, but it was still thick and mainly dark. There was a pattern too across his own defined abs. He did look good. I tried to inspect more, before it became too obvious. Someone else with European tastes, I thought, as I looked down at Donaldson's well-filled shorts.

He got up when he heard me approaching. This time he hugged me really close. He kissed me on the lips. Not long, just gently, as if it was the most natural thing in the world. No other man had ever kissed me like that before, yet it seemed entirely right. I felt the hair of his chest and stomach against my own, relatively hairless, naked and clean flesh. It felt so good to have the proximity of another body. I could feel my cock starting to respond again.

I shifted, backing away from him as discretely as I could, so my apparent excitement wouldn't be too obvious.

It wasn't very successful. He put a hand on each of my shoulders and held me at arms' length, looking me up and down.

'You look good, Andrew,' he said, 'well preserved.'

I smiled.

'For my age,' I replied. 'There is room for improvement.'

Donaldson smiled too.

'We can help,' he said.

I smiled again, accepting his generosity as an indication of care from an old friend.

'And you're dressed correctly too,' he said. 'I don't like many clothes inside the house. You don't mind that, do you?'

I shook my head.

He patted another chair, indicating that I should sit down beside him.

'Some wine for Professor Torrington, Luke,' he said.

'Donaldson,' I said.

'Yes?' he answered, looking directly at me.

'I'm retired now,' I told him. 'I've asked Luke to call me Andrew, I hope you don't mind, only he won't. He's calling me Andrew Sir.'

Donaldson smiled.

'I like that,' he said. 'It has an almost Indian ring to it, as if he was calling you "Sahib".'

I felt a little embarrassed then. My discomfort was clearly apparent to Donaldson.

'That's fine,' he said quickly, trying once again to put me at my ease. 'If you're happy with it, then I am. As you'll have noticed, Luke very much does as he is told.'

'I he a student?' I asked. I was curious to know more about this deferential young man.

'He was,' Donaldson replied. 'He's graduated now and staying with me for the summer. We'll see what happens then. I don't know how long you're staying, but if you're here more than a few days, you'll probably meet some of the other boys too.'

I hadn't been listening that carefully, but something in the way he said 'boys' caught my attention. I could almost hear the quotation marks. I was puzzled, unsure how to react. Donaldson noticed my uncertainty.

'Look Andrew,' he said. 'We're both grown men. We've known each other for many years, very many years. I have nothing to hide from you. If Mary was with you, well, I probably wouldn't have Luke running around quite so scantily clad; he'd be more formally presented, probably in black trousers, white shirt and tie, you'd see him as my butler, nothing more, nothing less. However, as you will have realized clearly by now, there is a lot more. And there are others. They perform similar services and roles for me. I like having them around. I like their bodies. I like watching them work their bodies. I like having them look after my body. I like having them do as I want, how I want, when I want. I give them some structure in their lives, help them establish some discipline for themselves. It works very well.'

I was sure that it did. There was something about the concept which was intriguing me. I wasn't sure exactly what though. The eroticism and sensuousness, the unashamed openness of it was a breath of fresh air in my life, I knew that. I had the suspicion that I faced some serious thinking. I hoped it would be okay, appropriate to talk to Luke, and find out more about him, and why he was doing what he was.

I took another sip of the Chardonnay as I thought for a moment.

'And the formality?' I asked Donaldson.

'It's all part of what's going on he said, a very important part. You said you had established what Luke was going to call you. I assume he has looked after you in your room?'

I nodded.

'Yes,' I said, 'he had.'

Donaldson thought for a moment.

'When when one of the others arrives, Andrew, I'll assign him to you. Is that okay?'

I nodded again. 'I don't see why not,' I said.

Donaldson noticed my slight hesitation.

'Look Andrew,' he said, 'you know that there is no obligation for anything sexual. I like my home to be erotic. You've always taken care of yourself and I don't think you have any objection to looking at bodies which are nicely taken care of.'

I smiled.

'Thank you, Donaldson,' I agreed, relaxing into this unfamiliar, but enticing, liberation.

Donaldson reached for my hand. There was certainly a far greater intimacy and candor between us than there had ever been before. Circumstances had changed, of course. It seemed silly for me to balk against this new experience.

'Come to think of it,' Donaldson said, 'I don't even know about your orientation, Andrew, not that that means much these days. I don't think I'm being too presumptuous if I say that I consider you a sensualist. Is that right?'

His observation surprised me, not because he had made it, but because it was so perceptive. He'd noticed aspects of me that, if I had noticed myself, I had put to one side, filed away in the innermost cells of my brain. If that was denial, it hadn't been a conscious, deliberate denial.

'You're making me think, Donaldson,' I said, 'but then you always did.'

He laughed.

'Just as long as you're comfortable,' he said.

It was my turn to reach for his hand. I squeezed it.

'I feel comfortable, Donaldson,' I said. 'I'm not quite sure why. All this is new to me. Yes, Luke is amazing. He looks so good. He's so polite and well- trained. He was even picking up my underwear with his mouth. Yet, I feel comfortable. It's nice to be sitting here, just wearing so little. That's nice. You look good too, Donaldson. I hadn't appreciated before just how well formed you were, but, well, I don't think I'd ever been in a situation where I could have found out.'

The more I said, the more I felt I had to think. I'd some idea of lifestyles like Donaldson's, but I'd never thought I knew someone who lived such a life, certainly not that I knew someone so well as Donaldson. I was confused too. I'd read about SM, of course I had. During the 1980s and 1990s, it had become hard to miss. It had become a mainstream topic of media interest, from broadsheet newspapers to lifestyle magazines. I'd seen men – and women – dressed from head-to-toe in leather and metal. There were years when it had been hard to avoid pictures of some of San Francisco's more outlandish street fairs on the TV news.

I had to think about my own sexuality too. I hadn't thought much about sex for many years. It hadn't been too important a part of my life. I'd become so engrossed in my own thoughts that I'd forgotten about Donaldson. I was a little startled when he touched my arm.

'A penny for them? Your thoughts?' he said.

I hesitated a moment. He was being supremely open about aspects of his own sexuality with me. I felt safe returning the favor.

'I was thinking about my sexuality,' I said.

Donaldson's eyebrows rose. 'You don't have to tell me anything if you don't want to, if you don't feel comfortable, if you don't trust me,' he said.

'It's not that,' I said, 'none of it. I do trust you, Donaldson, just as you trust me, by bringing me here, showing me this part of you, this important aspect of your life, your being. It's just that I'm not sure quite what there is to tell,' I said, honestly. 'I'd got to realizing that sex hasn't been that significant in my life for many years. Mary and I were more like brother and sister, close friends and companions for the last twenty years. Sex wasn't a part of our relationship. We had our own beds, our own rooms. We did other things. Sure, yes, I did jerk off, but not that often. I can't say that I thought of a human image as I did. I thought about the sensation and the orgasm. I'd seen some of the problems with affairs, especially with students. I'd seen the diseases, the unwanted pregnancies. I had intimacy with Mary, but that was beautifully different. It was sitting with her, reading on a winter's evening, arms around one another. There was a security, a comfort in each other. There was love, never sex.

'Mary had raised the subject a few times, at first. I was the one who wanted the distance. She'd suggested finding someone else, or buying it. I had been too uncomfortable to deal with it. It was good of her. It was typical too, she was so selfless. She'd expected it to have been far more important in my life than it had been.'

'And now?' Donaldson asked, asking the discrete question necessary to take my thinking forward.

'And now?' I repeated.

'I'm not sure, not sure at all,' I said. 'This is the first time I've been anywhere where I could think about it, Donaldson. It's the first time since Mary died that I have thought about it.'

I smiled.

'That won't do you any harm,' he said. 'It sounds as if it is almost something entirely new for you.'

Donaldson smiled too, laughing. 'But please don't think that what happens here is representative or commonplace. It isn't. It's quite rare.'

I nodded.

'Sure some of what I do, what Luke and the others do, isn't that unusual, but I try to make this a way of life, not just something which happens on pre-arranged evenings or at weekends.'

It was my turn to nod again. 'I understand,' I said.

Donaldson let me think for a few minutes more.

'I don't wish to pressure you, Andrew,' he said, 'but I'm really curious to know what you think. It's not often I have someone who's a complete newcomer, a virgin even. I'm curious to know what you think. I hope I'm not prying too much, but I'm genuinely interested.'

I paused. I wanted to look around but my eyes were focused on Donaldson's feet. I had to concentrate hard to persuade my gaze to travel up his body, until I was looking into his eyes.

'It's strange, Donaldson,' I said. 'My preconceptions were of leather, men in cages, in bondage, being whipped, but there seems to be a wonderful paradox here. You are comfortable. Luke is comfortable, but there is a formality, a discipline. I'm an outsider, yet I feel welcome. I don't feel embarrassed. I have to admit it, but I have even felt turned on.'

Donaldson nodded, his expression encouraging me to talk more.

'I don't think it's just me, Donaldson,' I went on. 'There's something else.' I was struggling for words. 'I don't know why, I can't find the evidence that makes direct, overt sense to me, but I get the impression that Luke loves you very much, very dearly indeed. I think,' I said, taking a breath before I continued, 'that you are a very fortunate man indeed.'

Cole

'You're right, Andrew,' Donaldson said, 'about Luke. He does love me. It's a very special love, but no doubt he'll tell you all about that himself, in time.'

'I'd like that,' I said.

'And you?' he asked.

'What about me?' I responded, almost petulantly.

'How are you feeling now?' Donaldson asked.

I took another sip of the Chardonnay. I appreciated its quality, letting it run around my palate before I spoke.

'Donaldson,' I said, 'I feel more relaxed yet more sexual than I have done in a very long time. I could get to like this life,' I said. I hadn't realized that I wasn't entirely joking.

'Perhaps you could get yourself a boy – or perhaps even a girl – in due course, Andrew,' Donaldson said, 'though I prefer boys. I could even perhaps send someone to you for a while if you wanted.'

I must have looked a little disconcerted.

This was all moving very fast.

Donaldson noticed my reaction.

'Of course, if you don't want it, there doesn't have to be any sexual contact between you. The boys know that. They accept it from the outset. They appreciate that they will be working domestically, that I'll probably use them in the playroom, I may cage them or beat them, yes,' he paused, letting me appreciate that there was a physicality to his life too. 'I do do that too, that I may oversee their workouts, and I will certainly punish them if what they do isn't good enough – for themselves or for me – but they also realize that any sexual contact is a bonus. It's more likely to be a treat, a reward for being good.'

'Thank you,' I said. Some of what Donaldson had said didn't matter to me. I was becoming more and more intrigued by the thought of another man's body. I wanted the touch of another man's flesh against mine. I wanted him to touch me, to stimulate me, to remind me of the joy that the millions of nerve-endings could produce. I suddenly wanted to touch another man's cock, to examine it closely, to check, to confirm that other men experienced the same sensations and feelings that I could. I was starting to dream. I suddenly realized that my cock was hardening inside my own tight swim briefs. The overt but casual eroticism of the setting was getting to me.

Donaldson got up and moved away. He said nothing. He left me with my thoughts, my dream. I closed my eyes. I felt the warmth of the evening sun on my body. It was good, beautiful, caressing me. Suddenly, I was no longer a retired professor, no longer fifty-six, but a teenager of sixteen. I remembered something suddenly that I hadn't thought about for decades.

I felt my mouth opening, becoming dry. I remembered that summer, in the Fifties. I remembered our small town, the school, but most of all I remembered Mary's brother, Cole.

Mary and I had been sweethearts, we used that word back then, all through high school. We'd found solace in each other, even then. I suppose the wedding bells really started ringing when we were only ten or eleven years old. Our folks were friends and they encouraged us. Her Mom and Dad liked me and mine felt Mary was the daughter they'd never had. Looking back, it was almost incest.

I'd forgotten about her brother. Perhaps I'd wanted to push him out of my mind. Guilt? Denial? It doesn't matter, now. I was trying to think where it was when I first encountered Cole. It was after swimming or sports. I was changing. He was a year older than I was.

He'd just been accepted into the Marines. The military was a stock route out of a small town in those days. For some reason, the Army or Navy didn't appeal to him. It had to be the Marines. He'd worked hard for it. He was certainly into himself. He worked out every day. He'd fallen for movies and the stars too, but it was only the men, and some particular men, who won his admiration. Cole wore tee-shirts that seemed to get tighter and tighter as he got bigger and bigger. He'd had his hair cropped, Marine style. He stood out because of that.

It must have been after swimming. Cole was just about to put on his tee-shirt when I noticed that the small of his back was still damp.

The memory was flooding back to me.

I remember calling out.

'Hey, Cole,' I'd said, 'you've missed a spot.'

I'd taken my towel and wiped the drops from near his kidneys. It was a magic moment. It was the first time I'd really appreciated the firmness of his teenage flesh, the dimples in his tight butt, the definition and curves of his shoulders and upper back. I remember stopping motionless, spellbound by the contact. I remember the suddenness of my own erection and the speed with which I'd dropped the towel, trying to make it fall as carelessly as possible to hide my cock.

I remember Cole turning, saying 'thank you' and then noticing the tent pole under the towel.

'You like what you see and feel?' he'd asked.

I hadn't had time to be embarrassed. I don't even think I was aware of quite how my body and mind were reacting.

He'd reached for me and pulled me back towards him. He'd taken my hand and placed it on one of his pecs. I'd been amazed by its firmness. He'd reached down, under the towel and touched my cock. It was the first time anyone else, let alone another guy, had done that. Sure, I'd jerked off, who didn't? Okay, this was the 1950s and we'd been told, time and time and time again that it was bad, a sin, that it would make you blind, deaf or both, and that you'd end up in hell, but that sure didn't stop us from doing it.

Cole had taken my hand and placed it on his cock. He was hard too. It was big, bigger than mine. I remember my mouth falling open.

I remember what he said.

'I think we need to do something about these, Andrew, don't you?'

I'd nodded, not quite sure what he had in mind.

'Your folks home?'

I'd shaken my head. 'No,' I'd said, 'not for a while.'

We'd finished dressing quickly. I can remember sweating in anticipation, hoping my erection wasn't too obvious under my pants as we walked from the school back to our house.

'We've got about half an hour,' I'd said to Cole as we went up the stairs to my room.

He'd taken the lead. I'd started to take my shirt off as soon as I'd closed the door, but he stopped me. He'd taken control. He stood me, almost at attention and carefully, gently took of my shirt. He stroked my body. It was the first time anyone had touched me like that. The sensation was almost overwhelming. Cole pulled his tee-shirt over his head and came and stood close to me, our bodies touching. I started running my fingers gently up and down his back, tracing the outlines and edges of the muscles I could feel. I bent forward. I didn't want to kiss him, but it seemed perfectly natural to start licking the firm flesh.

I remember him undoing my pants and pushing them down my legs, letting my erection spring free into the warm air. I fought for his pants too. I remember his cock pushing through the fly of his boxers. I had to struggle to get it back through, so I could pull the white cotton shorts down his firm, defined thighs. I remember running my hands round his back and feeling the firmness of his buttocks. They were so round, so pert. I rubbed my cock against his thigh. I licked the muscle of his upper chest.

Then, he reached for my balls. He gently put his fingertips to the back of the sac and ran them gently forward. I could hold myself no longer. I threw my head back, my mouth dropped open and I shot. The cum sprayed the side of his body. He held me close. He pushed my head to the cum. I don't to this day know why, but I felt as if I had in some way defaced some of his classic beauty. I bent and started licking my cum from his body.

I could feel him pulling on his own cock now. His breathing was getting quicker and deeper. His muscles were tensing. I licked harder, working my tongue across his abdomen to tickle his belly button. It was hard. His hand was banging against my chin. I'd moved a fraction upwards when he shot. His cum hit my chest. It felt so warm. I could feel it starting to run down me. I started rubbing it in, like an expensive ointment.

I remember lifting his hand and licking some of his cum from his fingers. We were still panting, short of breath, and although we'd pulled our pants back up into place, we our shirts were still on the floor when we heard the door. My mother was home.

I hoped we weren't too obviously red and flushed as we walked down the stairs. Mom knew Mary and accepted Cole, because he was her brother, without question. I'd given him my atlas, a treasured birthday present. He needs it for a class report, I told Mom. I think she believed me. Being with him probably looked like no more than extending existing family links; at least, I hoped that's what Mom thought.

Cole and I looked at each other sometimes after that, but nothing was ever said. He was a hot guy, I remembered. I remembered too that Cole was with us no more. He'd been killed in Vietnam. He'd climbed through the ranks of the Marine Corps and become an officer. He was a rising star when he died.

When I opened my eyes, Donaldson was standing over me, looking down. My cock was still hard. The thoughts of Cole's demise hadn't overcome the excitement the memory of my one and only encounter with another man had caused. Donaldson was well aware of my arousal.

'Whatever you were thinking, it must have been good,' he said, 'but you're going to have to leave it for a while. Dinner's ready.'

I closed my eyes for a fraction of a minute and and savored the grin that I knew was beaming from my face.

'I was remembering something very, very special,' I said as I got up.

I was about to put my hand into my briefs to re-arrange myself, as much for modesty as for comfort. Then I realized that this was probably the one place where I didn't have to do that.

I picked up my glass and walked with Donaldson towards his dining room. I could feel the head of my cock still pressing against the waistband of the swim briefs, trying to escape. I reached out for Donaldson's arm and held it while we walked the few paces.

So much, I thought, for the shirt and the shorts on the bed upstairs. For an instant, I knew I still had to lose more conventional uptightness if I was going to stay here long.

'It was when I was sixteen,' I said. 'I knew Mary then, of course, but it was before we were married. It was her brother. He was killed near Saigon'

This time I could feel the tears welling up more. Donaldson patted the hand I had curled around his arm.

'So,' he said, pausing and turning to look me directly in the eye, 'you're not quite the virgin I took you to be, Andrew.'

He bent forward and kissed me on the lips. I felt very loved, valued, very special.

It was my turn to pat him.

'Thank you.' It was all I needed to say.

Andrew's seduction

I enjoyed that dinner, said Andrew, as he continued relating his memories, taking his time as he thought, and then spoke.

Donaldson and I had been across the dining table, facing one another, said Andrew. He was still wearing his square-cut shorts, I was in my Speedos. Luke served us beautifully. He'd changed his swim briefs for a jockstrap, but there was a square panel of material hanging down the front, like an apron. He'd also put a leather thong around each of his biceps and around his forehead. He looked very beautiful.

'You know,' Donaldson said, 'how some people have reproduction sculptures, David or other Michelangelo pieces, in miniature?'

I nodded.

'Yes,' I said.

'I prefer my sculptures to be living, they're so much more beautiful.'

I grinned. I had to agree with him. Luke's sensuousness was getting to me.

'Are you deliberately trying to arouse me, Donaldson?' I asked, looking him directly in the eye.

He held my gaze for some seconds before answering. 'Let me say,' he said, pausing, 'that I am providing a situation where you can be aroused without embarrassment.' He smiled. 'I can't do any more or any less than your brain wants to let you.'

I had to nod. He had a point there. Was it because I was on the rebound? Was it the lack of sexual activity catching up with me? Was I genuinely turned on by Donaldson, Luke and this majestic way of life? I could feel the questions building up. I had to be patient. If I was to rush, I'd never find the answers. I'd find frustration instead.

'Perhaps,' Donaldson said, 'you do have some catching up to do after all, Andrew?'

Perhaps, I thought, I did.

Donaldson reached for my hand.

'Perhaps, despite Mary, and with all your love for her, it was her brother who made the circle complete?' he asked.

I pulled my hand away. It felt too fast. Yet, yet, again, the pieces were falling into place. Cole did mean something. It wasn't just the horniness of the memory. I moved my hand back.

'Donaldson?' I said.

'Yes, Andrew?' he answered.

I closed my eyes. 'I think you may be right.' I said. I paused. 'And, I'm scared.'

Donaldson looked at me. 'You can have as long as you want,' he said. 'It's been a long day.'

It had certainly been a tiring day. With flying from west to east, it had been a few hours longer than usual, but I seemed to have been running the gamut of emotions. In that way, yes, he was right, it had been a long day.

We sat quietly on the deck again after dinner. Luke served us coffee and a little whisky. It was still warm enough for none of us to have to worry about clothes. There was some noise in the distance. I gently rubbed each arm, my chest and my body with my hands. The near- nakedness felt very liberating.

'There's the gym in the barn, don't forget,' Donaldson said, as if reading my thoughts again, 'if you want to use it.'

I hadn't worked out in years. I usually got my exercise from walking or riding a bicycle.

'You have a good body, Andrew,' he said, 'you could make it even better.'

I smiled. No one, I thought, let alone another man, had ever paid me a compliment like that.

It wasn't too late when I made my excuses and went to my room. Luke had turned down the bed. My toothbrush was in a mug in the bathroom, my toiletries laid out. Deliberately, I left my swim briefs on the floor where I stepped out of them. My cock was still half hard. I was lying under a sheet when Luke came and knocked on the door. I'd left it ajar. I hated sleeping behind a closed door.

'Yes,' I said and he came in.

'Is there anything you need, Sir?' he asked.

I shook my head.

He walked across the room. I watched. His pace was deliberate. It wasn't too slow, but it wasn't hurried either. He had a bearing to him. He took pride in his movement. He ignored my gaze as he knelt and picked up the Speedos with his lips and took them to the laundry basket.

'There is a supply for the house, Sir,' Luke explained. 'If you wish, I will put some out for you for the morning?'

He looked at me now.

I nodded.

'That would be nice, Luke,' I said, 'thank you.'

His actions had made my cock hard again. For a moment, I closed my eyes. When I opened them again, he was kneeling beside the bed. His skin seemed to clean, strong and fresh. His head was bowed. I was confused. Here was this young man; he was offering himself to me. I wanted him, but I couldn't help think of Donaldson, his generosity, his hospitality. Did it include the most personal and intimate services of this beautiful young man? I reached out for his shoulder. He looked up.

'Yes, Sir?' he said, looking me directly in the eyes, almost defiantly.

'Is this okay?' I asked, 'do you have, er, permission?' I felt awkward, clumsy, asking the question.

'Yes, Sir,' he said, 'I do.' He paused.

'The Master has said I should provide whatever you want, Sir. Anything.'

He'd lifted his hands from his sides towards my shoulders.

'May I, Sir, please?' he said, looking as if he was about to start massaging me. I couldn't deny myself, or him, the contact any longer. '

'Yes, Luke,' I said, 'you may.'

I closed my eyes. The young man was visually so beautiful, but it was the sensation of touch which had, at that moment, become most important to me. I closed out the dominance of sight. I could feel him lift himself to stand and bend over me, allowing himself to reach across me more easily. I could feel him start to stroke and then knead my chest. He pulled the sheet down, away from me. I no longer cared about the erection pointing skywards.

He brushed my arm with his jockstrap. I could feel his cock pressing against the material. I grinned. Oh, I thought, this was so good. I lost all concept of time. Luke was amazing. He massaged my torso, my thighs, my chest, but despite my erection, he never made any contact with my cock or balls. It was as if he was teasing me.

Then suddenly, the sensation changed. Instead of his fingers, his tongue was stroking, licking, tickling my nipples. Slowly, deliciously, with his tongue, he traced a line from my calves, to my knees, to my thighs, to the ridge of skin between my ballsac and ass, again avoiding all contact with the sac itself or my cock. He moved his tongue teasingly across my stomach, into my belly button, up my sides to my armpits and back to my nipples.

Eventually, he began to concentrate on my groin. He licked around my sac, between my thighs and sucked on my hair. It felt so good. I wanted to come, but I didn't want to spoil the symphony of sensations Luke was orchestrating with his tongue and fingertips. He was playing me like the most precious and revered of musical instruments.

It took me a moment to realize that he had stopped. I could feel his breath though, on my cock. He was blowing gently onto the head. I hardly heard him when he finally asked the question.

'May I, Sir, please?' he asked.

I nodded. It took concentration to make any sound.

'Yes, Luke,' I whispered, 'you may.'

I have no idea how long he took, but that man took me on probably the most beautiful and significant sensuous journey of my adult life. "From blowing gently on my cock head, he ran the tip of his tongue from the back of my ballsac to the head. He licked it. The contact was minimal but the sensation was immense, intense; intense beyond belief. He licked my ballsac. He took each ball into his mouth, one at a time. He took both. He massaged the balls with his tongue and his gums. He squeezed them gently, then building intensity, letting go, building more and relaxing, against the roof of his mouth. I closed my eyes to best appreciate his ministrations.

He took the head of my cock to the back of his mouth, into his throat. He just held it there, motionless. He kept his mouth still and started a swallowing action, creating the most spectral of sensations on the head of my cock with the muscles of his throat. He licked up and down the underside of the shaft as he kept the head in his throat. He even tickled my ballsac. He ran his tongue in and out of my piss slit, time after time.

I'd never experienced anything like it. I was breathing deeply and long when the sensation caught me by surprise. I felt the muscles in my legs tightening. I stretched out my feet. I reached and held Luke's head, a hand almost over each ear. I pushed him down onto my cock as far as he could go. Then, I started pumping.

The orgasm hit me. I was born again. I let go of Luke's head. I could feel my hands reaching for my own temples, then describing an arc over my own head. I pulled air into my lungs as far as it would go. Never, at any time, did Luke move. My cock stayed, almost rooted, in his throat. I could feel him working away with his tongue, using the pressure to encourage the final drops of cum up my urethra. It was only when, at last, he felt my erection starting to subside that he moved his mouth up my cock, pausing only to lick the final drops of semen from the lips of my pisshole.

He kissed the head of my cock, each ball, my abdomen, each nipple and then me, gently on the lips.

'Thank you, Sir,' he whispered. I reached out for his hand. He let me hold it. I was close to sleep but tears were welling in the sides of my eyes. I felt Luke pull the sheet carefully and gently up my body.

* * *

I had no idea of the time when I woke. It took me a moment or two to remember where I was. I blinked, getting more accustomed to the light. The drapes had been pulled back and there was a glass of fresh orange juice on the nightstand beside me. I smiled. Luke had already been busy. I pulled myself up the pillows. I could see out of the windows, across the lush Pennsylvania countryside. Donaldson had chosen a wonderful site for his home, right on the edge of the city. It was close to amenities but also had great privacy.

I don't know how long I had been looking out at the fields and woods before I realized that Luke was standing in the doorway. I smiled.

'Good morning, Andrew, Sir,' he said.

I nodded and he came into the room.

'Did you sleep well?' he asked.

I smiled and nodded again.

'Very,' I said, 'thank you. Better than for a while.'

'The Master has some classes today and has already left,' Luke said. 'There is some breakfast downstairs, Sir, unless you would like me to bring you something up on a tray?'

I shook my head. I paused, looking around, appreciating my surroundings. A smiled crossed my lips.

'No, Luke, thank you,' I said, 'I think it would be better if I got up.'

It was his turn to nod.

'The Master said I was to make myself available, if you wanted to go anywhere, do anything, Andrew, Sir. He won't be home until late this afternoon.'

'What would you do if I wasn't here?' I asked him directly.

'I would do my chores this morning, Sir, then workout and probably go to the store for some groceries early this afternoon, Sir.'

I thought for a moment.

'Then,' I said, 'that's what I'll do too. I'll have some breakfast while you do your tasks, Luke, then we can workout together. I'll come with you to the store, if you have no objection?'

I knew that he wouldn't, probably couldn't, say no to me without disobeying Donaldson's orders. I wanted to establish a friendship, to talk to this man more. I respected him. I wanted to be courteous too.

I pulled myself further up the bed.

'A shower, Sir?' Luke asked.

I nodded.

He went into the bathroom and started the water.

I drank some orange juice; the sharpness helping my waking. Luke was standing by the bathroom door as I made my way towards the shower. I thought I could see his cock growing inside the light yellow Speedos that he was wearing that morning, but I couldn't be sure. I was about to walk passed him, but stopped. I turned and, surprising him, kissed him briefly on the lips before he could object and stop me.

'Thank you,' I said. 'Last night was very beautiful, Luke.'

I tapped his thigh and walked through to the shower.

I breathed deeply and thought while the warm water ran down my body. My own cock was hardening. I wondered what was happening to me. I'd been almost asexual for two decades. I'd never really thought about sex at all. I certainly hadn't considered myself as really having a sexual identity. I didn't identify myself as heterosexual because I didn't have sex. I didn't think about it much. Yet here I was not only finding that the sexual scales had fallen violently from my eyes, I was also discovering the beauty and joy of male bodies. Was I gay? I didn't think I was camp or effeminate. I giggled under the water. I didn't think I fell into any of the cultural stereotypes. I didn't know any show tunes. I enjoyed opera, but I wasn't a fanatic. I didn't think I had any better or worse taste than anyone else. I had no special interest in clothing, design or decor.

I decided I'd go with the feelings of the time. It may just be the novelty, I thought, the circumstances and the surroundings. I'd been in Donaldson's home less than a day. Everything could well change as soon as I left such a highly-charged sexual ambiance. I ran my hands up and down my body as I remembered the ecstasy that Luke had created for me the night before. I'd never experienced anything like it in my life.

I was still thinking about that orgasm as I stepped out of the shower.

Luke was waiting there for me with a towel. He'd started rubbing my back before I could take it from him.

'Luke,' I said, 'I really do appreciate this, but do please

remember that I'm not accustomed to it. I do have to go home sometime. Much as I love being spoiled, please don't pamper me too much.'

He smiled.

'I'll be getting your coffee then, Sir,' he said, grinning as he handed my the towel. I shaved and cleaned my teeth while I remembered. When I got back into my room, the bed had been made. On it were laid out two pairs of Speedos, one in light yellow, exactly the same style and shade as the ones Luke had been wearing, another in blue and a pair of square cut shorts. I wasn't sure quite why, but I chose the light yellow.

I found Luke and breakfast on the deck when I went downstairs. He couldn't hide his smile when he saw that I'd chosen the light yellow. I noticed his reaction. 'It seemed right,' I said.

I sat enjoying the morning sunshine and reading the newspaper as Luke cleared breakfast away. His attention would have shamed the most professional of waiters. As soon as my cup was emptying, he would be there, offering me more, his Speedo pouch tempting right in front of my face.

As soon as it felt sensible, I swam. I could see Luke moving about inside the house, doing his work. I hadn't swum for a long time either, I thought. The water had been a little chill at first, but I soon felt warmer. I set a reasonable, but not hurried pace and tried to keep it as I went backwards and forwards up and down the pool. I knew from my daily walks that it was healthiest to try and do between eighteen and twenty minutes' activity if the benefits for the heart and circulation were to be felt. I could see the clock on the deck. I set myself a twenty-minute target.

There wasn't a lot I could do for that time other than

think. There was too much. I tried not to consider myself and where I was. I tried to think about the sunshine, the green of the countryside. I didn't succeed. I kept coming back to Luke and what he stood for.

I tried to imagine a naked young woman. I could form an outline in my mind's eye, but I couldn't create any detail. It was so long since I'd touched a woman, other than my non-sexual contact with Mary, that I felt I'd forgotten what was there. The silhouette kept changing sex too. It became male. The image that my mind created was almost too stereo-typical; I remembered the expression from a magazine or newspaper article – 'body fascism'. I smiled as I swam. My image had firm, defined pecs, exemplary abdominals, well-formed thighs and a tight butt. Even in the cool water, I knew my cock was hardening.

I did the twenty minutes. I was breathing harder when I'd finished. Luke had put out a towel for me. The sun had risen in the sky and the temperature had increased, even in such a relatively short time. I sat down and waited for my skin to dry. I closed my eyes. My 'mind's eye Adonis' was still with me. I smiled. I enjoyed the games my imagination was playing. Who, I thought, needs virtual reality if they have imagination?

The sense of someone, something, close beside me disturbed the reverie. I blinked, trying to focus against the bright light as my attention shifted from the imaginary to the real. Luke was at my side. I looked up. He was holding a small bottle.

'Sunblock, Sir,' he said. 'You'll need it.'

There was no stopping him.

Before I could speak, he'd poured some of the liquid from the bottle onto his hands. Almost instantaneously, he was gently kneading my shoulders, rubbing the cream into my skin.

He knelt so that he could work the liquid into my stomach and thighs. I could feel him teasing me, trying to caress my balls within the prison of their nylon pouch. He was trying to make the contact accidental, I felt, incidental. I tried to ignore him. My brain was only a little more successful than my cock. I turned over on the lounger when he reached my feet. I turned my face away from him and smiled as Luke paid particular attention to my butt, my inner thighs and hips.

I had to admit that I wasn't sure how to react. I was loving the attention, that was for sure. I was also loving the physical sensation, there was no doubt about that whatsoever. Something was jarring. It didn't seem quite right. I'd sorted out that Donaldson had given his approval. Luke didn't need any special permission to touch me or become intimate. I felt he was flirting with me.

There was at least that aspect to Luke's situation. I could ask directly. I'd wanted to maintain a friendship, a courtesy towards him, but I needed to know. The only way was to ask him, there and then.

'Luke,' I said, turning over to face him, 'I have something to ask you.'

He moved his hands away from me and put the top on the lotion bottle.

'Yes, Sir?' he said, cautiously. I smiled, making him wait for my question.

'Are you,' I said, making the words draw out, 'are you flirting with me, Luke?'

I grinned as he went red. I'd hit home. He didn't need to say anything. His body's response had given me the affirmative answer that I'd been looking for. I looked at him though. I wanted him to say it, to confirm it. His words came a moment later. He'd put his hands behind his back and his head was bowed. There was some shame and remorse now.

'Yes, Sir,' he said. 'I suppose I was.'

'That's what I wanted to hear,' I said. 'Thank you.'

It took a moment, but he raised his head and looked at me.

'Yes?' I said, starting to tease him.

'Is that all, Sir?' he asked.

'That's all,' I said.

Disappointment appeared in his eyes. I grinned. I didn't have the heart, or the experience, then, to draw out the gentle torment any longer.

'I appreciate the attention, Luke,' I said, 'I really do.'

He relaxed then.

A smile of pleasure started to form on his lips. He knelt back on his haunches.

'It's just that I'm, well, new to all this,' I said. I didn't want to justify myself to him, but an explanation might help me get to grips with thoughts that were nagging away at me, persuasive and lasting, but not unduly irritating.

'I don't know how to respond, what to say,' I said. 'I get the impression that I don't need to do anything for you, except simply accept what you have to give. Is that right?'

He nodded.

'But, Luke, you have to remember that I'm a lot older than you are, and that I have a background of sharing, of mutuality, of sex being something that two people enjoy together, simultaneously ....'

He looked at me, again as if he wanted permission to speak. That too was something I was having to get used to. I was, I hoped, learning sufficiently quickly how to read the signs. I nodded.

'It is mutual, Sir,' he said, quietly, as if he was choosing his words very carefully. 'You didn't touch me last night, Sir, but it was a wonderful experience for me too, Sir.'

It was my turn to look at him puzzled.

'I didn't need an erection, Sir, although I was hard all the time Sir. I didn't need to touch myself, Sir, or to cum. My pleasure came through you, Sir, feeling how your body was responding, how your muscles tensed and relaxed, how your erection increased, then subsided a little, increased more, how you squirmed when I touched your sides, Sir, I nearly came too when you held my head, Sir. It's about giving, Sir. I felt proud Sir, when I saw that smile on your face, Sir, even though your eyes were closed. I saw so much tension had left you, Sir. That was my pleasure, my privilege, my honor, Sir.'

The intensity of his speech and the honesty of his emotions surprised me. My own response surprised me too. I hadn't expected to understand and appreciate every word he said, but I did. Although the memories were old, distant even, I knew exactly what he was talking about. I put my hands to my face. I could feel the tears welling up inside me. Cole appeared in my mind's eye. I tried to think why. I didn't think I'd done that much to provide pleasure for him, on that one single occasion all those years before. I tensed my fists. I could feel my breathing getting faster. I licked my lips. I bit my bottom lip. I couldn't hold my emotions any longer, I let the tears flow.

I felt Luke move as I closed my eyes. Instead of kneeling beside me, he was standing, leaning on the back of the lounger, his arms around me. He took each of my hands in his. He rested his head on my shoulder, his mouth close to my ear. I felt him bend forward a little more and kiss my shoulder blade. I squeezed his hands.

'Yes?' Luke asked.

I didn't know anything about that question, yet instantaneously, simultaneously, I knew all of it, everything it encompassed.

'Yes,' I said.

I let go of Luke's hands. I reached out, moving my hands out away from me, describing a circle and flexing my fingers out from half-clenched fists, trying to represent physically the layers falling away. I tried to concentrate on the image in my brain. There was a circle, a sphere, it was black, but inside was the brightest, sharpest, most intense, yellow-white. It was as if the most powerful supernova of all time was exploding out of the deepest, darkest of black holes. I could see the debris flying off in all directions, yet there were rings as the reverberations of the metamorphosis sped outwards.

I lay back. I was panting. I was almost shivering, despite the warmth. Luke grasped my hands again and squeezed them. I could feel him smiling. I fought to open my eyes. I looked up and could see his face, upside down, above me.

He bent forward and kissed me on my lips.

'Welcome,' he said, 'to my world.'

We stayed close, like that, for quite a few minutes. It took some time for my breathing to return to normal. I'd heard him speak, but I hadn't taken in what he said. I let go of one of his hands and reached for my forehead. It felt hot. I felt very strange. I didn't realize until he was back, kneeling and handing me a glass of iced water that Luke had let go of me.

'Wow,' I said. 'That was something.'

The words seemed inadequate. I was aware that my heart was still beating faster than normal. There was a numbness in my arms. I felt my expression was glazed. I was grateful Luke was there. He reached for my hand and squeezed it again, continuing the reassurance.

I felt the tears welling again. I felt different. I wasn't me. I didn't know who I was, what I was. I felt that something had fallen away. It wasn't that there was a new purpose exactly, more as if a huge, thick metal shell had shattered, leaving a bright, clear, unspoiled nucleus unprotected, shining and bringing a new light and intensity to my life. I felt as if it had been there all the time, but that for years and years and years the layers of protective shell had been growing and solidifying. It was as if the deepest, purest part of my psyche had finally been discovered, had escaped. I grinned. I knew it was there; I didn't know what it was, or what it represented. I reached for a hand.

'Luke,' I said, plaintively, 'I'm scared.'

* * *

Luke sat with me. I don't know how long we were there. He sat on the deck beside me. Every so often, he would stroke me, or hold my hand. I was still nervous, my heart beating quickly.

I wondered what was happening to me. The last few hours seemed so intense. Had there been a transformation, I wondered? It was as if there had been, but I didn't think such things happened to people.

I was fifty-six, for goodness' sake, nice, white, respectably professional and middle-class. I was comfortably off, if not affluent. I was a widower. I was, I thought, relatively sane. Catharses like this didn't happen to people like me. They just didn't. It wasn't credible.

I knew of people who'd 'found' religion, a faith. Those experiences seemed to have been very dramatic, intense and sudden. This wasn't, I thought, religious though. I'd known people who'd discovered sex in later life, but that was conventional. It was screwing, usually with whores, the costs eating into their pensions.

I was re-bounding, I decided. It was a reaction to all the

changes, stopping working, then Mary's sudden death, dealing with the practicalities. That was it. Perhaps I didn't have anything to worry about, be scared about after all. I sighed.

I reached Luke's hand. He looked at me and smiled.

'Yes, Sir?' he said. There was a sparkle in his eye as he spoke.

I grinned.

'Thank you,' I said. 'Thank you for being here.' I could feel the tears building up again.

Here was this man, this young man, whom I hardly knew, whom I'd only met for the first time a few hours before, providing me with unconditional love and support. I didn't know him, but I knew too that there was, even then, an intimacy and a bond between us that would last for the rest of my life. It was yet another new experience.

My life had been one where you'd met someone, perhaps socially or professionally, then, very gradually, over time, you had sniffed them out, established whether they could be trusted, had dinner, circumspect conversations, exchanging gossip and some perfunctory personal thoughts and opinions. Intimacy, if it occurred at all, was reached only after years, sometimes many years, of contact. Donaldson was like that. We'd known each other more than twenty years, but our intimacy had now been established, even if it had only fallen into place in the previous few hours.

With Luke it was different. I didn't know him. I could see his body. I didn't know his second name, his age, or anything about him, but he had witnessed or created two of the most intense emotional experiences of my life within a few hours. I shook my head. My norms, my standard reference points were changing.

'Perhaps,' Luke said, 'we should do something?'

I didn't notice for a while, but for the first time, he hadn't asked me for permission to speak. I nodded.

'I need to work out,' he said.

I took a deep breath.

'I'll come with you,' I said.

I'd known earlier that it was a good idea, as I pushed myself up off the lounger, I knew it was even more important. I didn't know why, I just knew that it was.

Luke was in front of me when I finally got to my feet. He took each of my hands in his and held them at my sides. He came forwards towards me. The difference in our height was really apparent for the first time. I grinned. It was a strange reflection on our apparent roles, the house slave towering over the guest. He bent forward and kissed me firmly and deliberately on the lips. I wanted to melt.

I felt like a teenager in love as Luke held my hand and led me towards the old stable block. I felt carefree. My chest felt less stressed. It was a curious, unusual, sensation.

Andrew's awakening

My mouth fell open as I followed Luke into the stable building. There was a gym as impressively equipped as many professional facilities. There was a changing area and, to one side, a sauna.

I could see cupboards and lockers. At the far end of the gym was a double door.

'That's the dungeon, the play space,' Luke said, following my gaze. I must have looked puzzled. 'I'll show you later,' he said, smiling.

I was still looking around at all the pieces of equipment as Luke moved around, not paying much attention to what he was doing. As I looked more closely, I had started noticing that some of the equipment in the gym was not what would be found elsewhere. Beside a frame for squats there was a stool with a dildo impaled upon it. I smiled. I was beginning to understand more, both about Donaldson and about the way of life on his property. I wondered what it would be like to have one's ass penetrated. I expected that it would hurt, but if it hurt so much, how come so many people got so much pleasure from it? I'd have to swallow my innocence if I wanted to find out.

Luke regained my attention when he handed me a jockstrap.

'It's all I usually wear,' he said. 'You might like to too.'

I nodded. He started to push his Speedos down. I was mesmerized. I felt like an adolescent schoolboy, seeing another man undress for the first time, curious about the size and shape of another guy's cock and balls. My eyes were fixated. I felt so rude, but I was intrigued.

First I noticed that there was not a vestige of hair to be seen around Luke's cock and balls. I looked up and down him. There was no hair to be seen on his body at all. Then, I noticed the metal ring around the base of his cock and balls.

'It helps keep me hard,' he said, having followed my gaze.

'It's a cockring. It also stops my balls retreating.'

He came towards me.

'Andrew Sir,' he said, 'you are a virgin, aren't you?'

I was still standing there, almost statue-like, as he turned. I didn't move as he bent down and pulled my Speedos down my legs. He looked closely at my cock and balls. I watched as he walked across the gym, naked apart from the ring, his cock and balls bouncing in front of him as he went. I waited as he pulled the double doors open and disappeared into the darkness.

There were two rings in his hand when he got back to me.

He handed me one. I felt it. The material felt strange. It wasn't leather, or rubber.

Luke noticed my curiosity.

'Neoprene,' he said, 'what wetsuits are made from. It's just elastic enough and comfortable. Now, pull one ball through at a time, then your cock.'

I didn't have any trouble with the balls, but my cock had started to harden again with the contact. Luke grinned. He reached for the sides of the band and pulled them apart. The elasticity was such that I could push my growing erection through. He let the ring close gently. It felt good. He smiled. He took the jockstrap from my hand and knelt down. I stepped into it and he pulled it up. It took a little adjustment, but he soon had my erection hard against my stomach and my balls comfortably resting in the pouch. I caught sight of myself in a mirror. The outline looked obscene but at the same time beautiful. Luke smiled again.

I was catching up with so much so quickly. I'd swum that morning for the first time in a long while. I tried to remember when I'd last used a gym. I couldn't. I knew that I shouldn't be too ambitious.

In reality, I did very little more than play with a few weights that morning as Luke worked out. The young man's routine had certainly been serious but the way in which he'd behaved had not been. I'd been silent until he started to find the going hard.

'Go on,' I said, 'you can do it.'

I was surprised when he stopped.

He put the weights down and turned to face me.

'If you're going to encourage me, Andrew Sir,' he said pointedly, 'then at least do it with conviction, please.'

He looked at me challengingly, but at the same time there was a gleam in his eye.

I moved towards the bench where he was sitting.

'I take it you mean that, young man,' I said.

We were both teasing each other now.

He nodded. '

Okay,' I said, 'how many reps are you doing?'

He paused. He looked as if he wanted to set himself a hard target, but at the same time, there was a need for caution.

'So how many?' I asked.

'Eight, this time, Sir,' he said.

I nodded and moved to stand over him.

The sight facing me really was exceedingly beautiful. Luke had closed his eyes to concentrate. I had a chance to inspect the flesh. Although the exercise he had already done was starting to have an effect, adding a tautness to his muscles, there was no denying the underlying form. Donaldson was correct when he had alluded to Michelangelo. Luke's body was defined, but without being burdened by the extra development that can backfire for some bodybuilders.

'Eight,' I said, as Luke lifted the barbell from its rest and pushed it up for the first time.

'Seven.'

I tried to put a determination and authority into my voice. I had to concentrate to do it.

'Six.'

I could see the beginnings of real effort starting to appear on his face, even though his eyes were closed.

'Five.'

I noticed that even though Luke was performing bench press exercises, his thighs were tensing.

'Four.'

The sweat was starting to appear on his forehead; his breathing was becoming faster and deeper.

'Three'.

The strain was becoming apparent. The upwards push was far slower, far harder than it had been.

'Do it, Luke,' I said. I chose my words carefully. I had to find the right tone of voice. I had to issue an order. It had an effect.

He found the power and straightened his arms.

'Two.'

He took a deep breath before starting to make the effort.

'Yes, boy, you can do it, boy. You will do it, won't you boy? You can do it, can't you boy?'

I hoped the teasing would work. I think it did.

His eyes flashed open for a second.

There was a defiance in them, but also a smile, a conviction and determination. I liked what I saw.

'And, one, Luke,' I said. 'Do it for your Master. Make yourself even more handsome boy, you know you want to, you need to.'

I looked down his body at that point. It took me a lot of concentration not to start grinning when I saw his jockstrap.

Despite the effort he was making with his arms, his cock was hardening. The strain was showing. The push upwards had slowed almost to a stop.

'Do it, boy,' I said, trying to muster as much authority as I could, 'do it, slave. You're not going to disappoint your Master, are you?'

I could see the tension in his face as he tried to push the bar upwards, inch by slow inch. I bent to put my hand close to the weights, just in case he did need help. It brought my mouth closer to him.

'Come on' slave boy,' I whispered. 'Do it for your Master.'

I watched carefully as he gritted his teeth. The strain showed across his chest, along the veins of his arms, in his legs and in his jockstrap.

He was concentrating hard. He didn't have much further to go before he could lock his arms straight, three inches became two. He was getting nearer the culmination – straight arms.

'Think of the pleasure you'll bring your Master, boy,' I whispered again.

Two inches became one. I could almost feel his heart beating.

'One final effort for your Master, boy, you're nearly there. Make yourself beautiful for your Master, boy. Come on. Yes, for your Master.'

He was at the most precarious point. He was straining to hold the heavy bar while trying to conserve the energy and build the determination for that final, almighty, push.

'Ready boy?' I said. 'Let's go for it, together, let's make that body beautiful. Think of what you're giving to your Master, Luke, think what I can tell him. Think of how he may enjoy seeing you do this, doing more, another day. Let's make that difference, Luke.

'Three,' I said,

'Two ... One. Go for it.'

He did. He shook his head as he made that final push. It was exquisite to watch. He did it. He held the bar for a moment, his arms extended. I watched the delicious agony on his face as his muscles responded during the weights' descent. He was piling on the intensity and the pain. He was doing it himself, making sure the effort and the strain were greatest as the weights were lowered to their resting place. He was panting hard now, his chest rising and falling as his lungs and heart strove to deliver the much-needed oxygen around his body.

He let his arms down carefully, almost in slow motion, as soon as the weights were on the rest and the burden had been lifted. His eyes were still firmly closed. The perspiration was growing on his brow.

I shifted my own position still more. I bent through the frame and kissed him briefly on the lips. The gesture surprised him. His body tensed, just for a fraction of a second, before he relaxed again, comfortable in knowing what had happened.

'That,' I said, 'was amazing. Delicious. I hope you are proud, boy. You have every reason to be.'

It took Luke a little while to recover. I used a rowing machine while he did. It felt nice only wearing a jock. I'd never had such freedom. I worked myself gently, turning occasionally to see how Luke was doing.

Eventually, he stood and walked towards me. He was still breathing hard. I stopped rowing and stood up. I hadn't noticed the showers next to the sauna when we came in. I watched as Luke bent to remove his own jockstrap. His cock was still showing the signs of his earlier erection.

I was about to take mine off when he knelt down in front of me and reached for the waistband with his mouth. I put my hands on my hips and looked down, watching as the young man again closed his eyes and went to work. His action had provoked my cock. It grew again and made the job that much more difficult. Luke had to pull hard to get the waistband open enough for my cock to escape from the pouch. He pulled the jock all the way down my legs without letting it go. When I'd stepped out of it, he stood up and put the garment on a locker. He smiled at me as he did so. I reached for him and kissed him again. Some might have found the action strange. I tried not to think about the whys and wherefores, but in the circumstances and the environment of Donaldson's household, it was highly appropriate, delicate and impressive. I reached for him, and held him by each shoulder, just as Donaldson had done to me the evening before, and kissed him again, directly firmly on the lips, looking straight into his eyes all the while.

My cock had surprised me. I was finding my sexuality. I appreciated the beauty of Chris's body and the deliciousness of his touch. My eyes were opening to the freedom of Donaldson's home. Yes, something deep inside me was reluctant, perhaps scared, but the bigger me was excited. I wanted that part of my psyche to triumph. I focused on that positivity, that desire for the erotic, the stimulating, the new. That's what I wanted.

Luke led me into the shower. He soaped me down, rubbing my back and legs before paying attention to himself. He toweled me first too.

We walked back naked to the house. It felt wondrous to be so free and to feel the warmth of the late morning sunshine on all of my body. I reached for Luke's hand. He looked at me, surprised. I raised the index finger of my other hand to my mouth. I didn't want him to say anything. I wanted the closeness, the security, the reassurance of the contact.

It didn't last long, just the few seconds it took us to reach the house.

Luke closed the doors behind us and locked them.

'Wait there, would you please?' he said as I started to make my way towards the stairs.

I nodded. I felt embarrassed then, waiting naked in the living room as he disappeared up the stairs. I could hear him moving around upstairs.

I was surprised when he came back down still naked. I had expected him to have dressed. He was carrying a small pile of clothes in one hand and two pairs of boots in the other. One pair was mine. I watched as he put the clothes down on a table and the boots on the floor.

I shook my head briefly. Although I'd been at the house less than a day, I was seeing, learning so much. Luke was still astonishing me. This time it was in how he bent to put down the boots. He kept his back straight and controlled his entire motion with his legs. It was a very elegant movement. It emphasized the curvature of his butt exquisitely, the arc running from his back towards his knees. Donaldson's description of a 'living sculpture' echoed in my mind.

I was still staring when he handed me the clothes. There was a polo shirt and some square cut shorts. There was an undergarment that I didn't recognize. It had a thong back, but the pouch was fuller than a g-string. The waistband was thick, about three inches, like that of a jock. I held it, curiously. Luke noticed my reaction.

'They're what dancers wear,' he said. 'They're amazingly comfortable; they hold you so well, there's never a movement. I love them.'

He smiled.

We both bent to put them on at the same time.

He was right. The pouch pulled the cock and balls up in a way that I'd never experienced before. I adjusted myself. I finally understood the mechanics which had held Rudolf Nureyev so firmly and deliciously. That man had been magnificent, in so many ways. I looked at Luke. His bulge too was simultaneously obscene and magnificent. He grinned. I knew exactly what he meant. The cockrings helped too. I couldn't help but wonder just how many lithe men used that technique too, to show off that little bit more on stage.

I knew, as I pulled on the shorts, tee-shirt and my boots that my erection was growing again. I hoped it wasn't too obvious as we went out of the front door and crossed the yard to the pick-up. I pulled the tee-shirt out of my shorts, where I'd tucked it in and let it flap, more discretely in front of me. I looked at Luke, questioningly.

'That's not something I'm allowed to do, Sir,' he said, grinning again.

* * *

The trip to the store finally gave me the chance I'd been waiting for to talk with Luke.

I'd smiled.

'Luke,' I'd said, 'tell me all about yourself, if you would please. I'm curious.'

I'd been thinking he could tell me as he drove, but that didn't seem such a good idea anymore. I was too curious to want him distracted.

'Luke,' I asked.

He turned and looked at me from behind the wheel.

'Yes, Andrew Sir?'

'I'm in charge now, right?'

He nodded.

'So, if I say I'd like to go for a coffee and I want you to come with me, you won't be in trouble with Donaldson?' I wanted to be sure. I didn't want him punished for my inquisitiveness.

'As I said, Andrew Sir, my orders are to please you.'

I instructed him to pull into the next coffee shop we saw. Despite the kids coming out of school, it was still quite quiet for an afternoon. Luke protested a little, but acquiesced when I insisted on paying. We found seats away from the others.

'I don't have any secrets from the Master,' he said after we'd sat down, 'not any more. It was part of the contract; no privacy.'

He looked at me.

'I hope you don't mind me saying this,' he said, 'but it still feels a little unusual for me. I have nothing to be ashamed about, but talking about my life, these aspects of me, my personality, still seem difficult.'

I nodded.

'I fully appreciate that,' I said. 'But you do have that order, don't you, that you don't have any privacy?'

It was Luke's turn to smile.

'That's true,' he said. 'To be honest with you, Andrew, I still don't know whether it is exclusive to the Master or a general instruction.'

I thought for a moment.

'Well,' I said, 'if it's any help, my curiosity is entirely personal and whatever you say to me won't go any further. I wouldn't even tell Donaldson.'

Luke turned his attention away from the road for a second.

'You mean that?' he said.

'Yes,' I said, 'I sure do.'

I caught some sense of unease.

'Perhaps even if protocol says that I should disclose or pass on some of your thoughts and comments to him, I think these are circumstances where such etiquette is probably best sacrificed.'

The statement seemed to reassure him.

Luke's attention was distracted by approaching customers for a second. I waited.

'What do you know?' he said when we were less likely to be overheard.

'Assume nothing,' I said. 'I met you less than a day ago. I know your name. I know what you look like. I know you were one of Donaldson's students. That's about it. As for age, most talents, experience, skills and so on, nothing. Run me through the résumé, Luke, personal and professional.'

'I've read the books,' he said.

I wondered what he meant. He noticed my confusion.

'There are books, storybooks, novels, about men who live this style of life, Andrew. They describe the psychology and backgrounds of people like me. I'm very like them, I think.'

Luke and Rob …

'I was brought up as an only child, by my father,' Luke began. 'My mother left us when I was five. They divorced. It was painful, I know. Even to this day, it still hurts my Dad to think about it. She moved away. She re-married. I have a half-sister somewhere, two, three years younger than I am, but I've never met her. I don't even know her name. It took me a long time – ten years in fact – to find out why Mom had left, so suddenly and with so much hatred.

'It happened when I was seventeen. I was with another guy from school. We were in my room. I was on my knees sucking his cock when Dad came home. We hadn't heard him come in. I think we'd left the door open or something. Anyway, he was back early, and was looking round to see if I was back from school. I was a keen student and he'd come to my room to see if I was doing my schoolwork.

'Neither Rob, my friend, nor I saw him. The door was ajar. I didn't even know he'd seen us until later. We'd had great sex. Rob had a great body, even then. He was almost stereotypical too. He was in the football team, the guy with the best physique, the biggest cock, the one who worked out most and hardest. He was always surrounded by the girls. They all had crushes on him, wanted to date him. Then, as soon as they got close, they'd get scared, he said. I wasn't sure. I can't remember why, but we'd started talking one day. I was something of a loner. I didn't have many friends. I was happy enough. I didn't avoid people. I wasn't a recluse or anything like that. I enjoyed some sports, but mainly those you did on your own. Team events, anything which involved dependence on others, felt alien to me. Already, even in my teens, I'd had to develop an ability to rely on my own resources. I was in reasonable shape. I'd swim and run. I'd even tried wrestling too. I'd workout sometimes too. Sure, I noticed some of the girls looking at me, comparing me with the other guys, but they were always in groups, pairs, threes, maybe, never on their own. I didn't like that.

'Perhaps not having anyone female around the house had affected me. I knew what maleness was like. I knew from my Dad the smells of masculinity. He was a big strong guy. Dad was probably the Rob of his day, the stud star of the football team. Dad managed a local leisure facility. There was a gym, tennis courts, a pool, plus a coffee shop, a restaurant, a golf course. It was like a country club, only not as exclusive. He was still a young man. He was about 40 when I was in my teens. I was proud of him. He was still firm and fit where other guys' dads had got flabby. He had a far bigger chest than me, but by the time I was 15 or 16, the same size waist. I'd felt more like a man the day he said to me that he didn't think I needed kid's clothes any more. I thought he was being smart, accepting that while money wasn't really tight, we still had to be careful. Such economies, I'd been raised to believe, were always worth making. What's saved in the short-term, Dad had taught me, usually paid off in the future. His philosophy, I later appreciated, was sound in several ways. Anyways, what was in his closet was mine, he said. I liked that. Sure, some of his tee-shirts looked like tents on me, hanging from my shoulders. I wore his jeans though. For a year or so, I'd have to turn up the legs, but, no problem, they still felt good.

'We shared lots. We'd do chores without thinking about them. Dad taught me to cook early on, while I was still a kid. It was basic, but good. I learned what was good for you – and bad. I learned what he didn't like. If I was home first, I'd cook for us. If he was, he did. We were often more like friends, brothers, than Dad and son. I liked that. We'd check each other's rooms; if there was laundry to do, we'd do it. Weekends, we'd share tasks; one of us would clean inside while the other swept the yard. Then, he'd become more like a Dad, spoiling me with some treat or other in the afternoon. We'd go out, walking, cycling, in a sail boat on the lake, just me and Dad.

'Dad didn't worry too much about clothes. I can't remember a time when I wasn't used to him being around the house naked. He liked shorts too, but he was happiest when it he could feel the air against his skin. He hated wearing shoes and socks too. He'd be barefoot whenever he could. I must have been about four, I think, Mom was still around. I think it must have been a summer weekend. He appeared in a bikini swim brief for the first time to go outside and clean the yard. Mom went mad. She said it was disgusting, showing himself off like that. She cursed him for displaying everything to the neighbors. He ignored her. She stormed out. He went to work. I remember sitting on the deck thinking how beautiful that rounded bulge looked. I remember seeing some pictures of pro wrestlers in a magazine. I'd be a wrestler, I thought, so I could get to wear briefs like that every day.'

We'd pulled into the parking area by the store. I followed as Luke led me towards a coffee shop. He'd started to tell his story. The groceries could wait.

'When I could, in my teens again, this is,' said Luke, 'I started wrestling at school. I'd been watching the older guys.

I loved the singlets and the bulges under them. I was given my first jockstrap and loaned a tight red singlet for my first lesson. I think the coach must have seen to that. I just remember that my growing cock had got so hard during that close contact with another guy, I'd been so embarrassed, scared that someone, anyone, would see my excitement that it was a few more years before I went back to it.

'I decided I liked jocks though. You know what teens are like, how you don't like to think of your folks as being sexual, let alone having sex? You know how you feel as if it's something new that you've discovered? That no one has ever done something before? I was like that. I thought I may be the first guy to find jocks sexy. Despite Dad's openness, I'd wear one most days, but I'd throw clean jockeys or ones that I'd worn for just a few minutes into the laundry. I was working Saturdays by then, filling shelves in the local supermarket. I'd save and buy a jock or some underwear that I'd seen advertised in a magazine. I'd keep them hidden, under the bottom drawer.

'I was so embarrassed the day Dad came out of his room one morning wearing one of my briefs. I hadn't realized that I'd left it out, with the rest of the laundry. I was confused. He looked so sexy, the curved outline of his heavy ballsac in the thin material, but I had to look away when he spoke. 'Hey, Luke,' he'd said, 'these are real good, real comfortable, why didn't you tell me about them?' I muttered something and fled back to my room. I was relieved nothing more was said. I'd felt red all day that day. Even in class, I thought I was blushing. I felt easier by morning when there had been no more comments. Dad hadn't criticized me. It took me a day or two more to realize that he'd actually complimented me. My confidence grew. I became more brazen. I added another pair to the laundry. I left them in the pile when they were dry. They disappeared one day and were back, worn, in the laundry basked the next. I washed them again and the same happened, but nothing was said.'

Luke chose the quietest corner of the restaurant. I didn't need to say a word as he kept talking. I listened intently. I gestured for coffees for us both as he went on with his story.

'I'm sorry,' he said, suddenly, 'this must all seem very disjointed.'

I shook my head.

'It's all part of what happened.' I shrugged. 'I appreciate that, Luke,' I said. 'Go on, please.'

He did, in his own words.

I'd first talked to Rob – you remember, the guy Dad saw me sucking – at the diner, Luke continued. It was a Saturday, after work. He'd been at a ball game and was on his way home, he said. It was a quiet time, that strange period in early evening when the most rebellious kids had obediently returned to the family fold, ready to come out again later for meals with their Moms and Dads. They'd been at the diner, drinking soda all afternoon, shouting about their rebelliousness and independence. The quieter, more conventional versions, would be back soon. I was enjoying that break, the lull between the two contrasting storms.

Rob recognized me. He looked tired. I knew I was. It had been a busy day. Dad was working late that night, there was a contest or something going on at the leisure facility. I hadn't wanted to cook at home on my own. I'd had my fill of stacking shelves that day, so, instead, I'd grabbed something to eat at the diner.

'You need company,' Rob said as he walked over with a soda.

I'd smiled. It was good to be noticed by the guy. I wondered what was most casual to say. I'd love that guy's company.

'Sure,' I said.

'Been busy?' he asked.

'Yeah, I started at seven, staking the shelves,' I said. 'I'm about to head home, I'm ready for it. You?'

He waited a moment, taking some of his drink, then looking down.

'A game ...' he said. I waited. I felt there was more. I remember the doubt; Rob looking at Luke and Luke looking at Rob. Both of us looking at each other – and then around, to see who else may be watching, or be within earshot. We relaxed at the same moment. The only other person in the diner was the owner, Mr Berg, and he was busy in the kitchen.

'Can I tell you something, Luke?' he asked.

I nodded. I tried to hide my surprise that he even knew, or remembered, my name.

'Sure you can,' I said.

'Something you'll tell no one else? Ever?'

I wondered what could be so serious, playing on his mind so much.

'Yes,' I said.

'You have my word.'

He looked at me defiantly, making sure that I was being honest with him.

'I mean it,' I added.

'He waited a moment more before he spoke. He seemed to be trying to work out whether it was safe to tell me.

'You're a loner, Luke, aren't you? Do you tell people your secrets?'

I thought for a moment before answering.

'I don't have many secrets,' I said, 'but I don't know many other people I'd tell, Rob, if that's what you're thinking.'

He looked around again.

'You won't tell anyone in school?' he asked.

'No,' I said, as firmly as I could. 'I won't tell anyone, in school or anywhere else. Not unless you say I can.'

He seemed more relieved then.

'It's Betty,' he said.

I knew Betty.

She was in his class, a girl who was best described as brassy. She was dominant, the strongest in the group. She was always with Rob. It was clear to everyone that while he was her guy, she wasn't his girl. I wondered what had happened. There were tears in Rob's eyes. I began to fear the worst. I could feel myself tensing. How could I ask? What could I say? This was a small town. There'd be hell to pay for all of them as soon as it became known. For the parents, it would be particularly horrid. The hatred, especially from the church, the last time one of the girls had got pregnant was so bad the family had upped and skipped town.

'She's not ...?' I found myself asking, looking up into Rob's eyes. It took him a moment to realize what I was asking.

He was shocked.

'Oh, no, Luke, not that, no way,' he said, strongly, unashamedly. 'It's not that at all.'

He relaxed a little.

'If anything,' he said, almost whispering, conspiratorial, 'it's exactly the opposite.'

I waited.

'I couldn't do it, Andrew. I couldn't.'

There were tears in his eyes. I didn't know if he realized what he was doing, but he'd reached across the diner table and was holding my hand. I hoped that no one came in.

I squeezed his hand. It seemed the right thing to do.

'May be this isn't the best place to talk,' I said.

He pulled his hand away, suddenly noticing what he'd been doing.

'Look,' I said, 'come with me. Dad's out, working. We can talk there. It's on your way home, Rob.'

He looked uncertain. He swallowed the last of his soda. Rob didn't have enough money to waste, even on a drink.

He was the first to stand.

I followed.

I called for Mr Berg and left money for the sodas on the counter.

I waved Rob away when he reached for his pocket, at least I'd been earning that day, I thought.

We walked slowly. Rob was pushing his bicycle. There was a far-away look in his eyes as we made our way along the side of the road.

The house was quiet when we got there.

I pulled two of Dad's beers from the icebox. Although I was under age, he'd said it was important that I should learn how to drink, sensibly and slowly, rather than run loose and irresponsible in the bars as soon as I was twenty-one.

Rob looked at me suspiciously when I handed him the beer.

'I'm allowed,' I said. 'You look as if you could do with one.'

I swallowed hard. How the hell did I know that? At seventeen?

I hoped that my act of confidence was holding.

'Come on,' I said, leading him to my room.

It had taken him a while to relax. I didn't know quite what to do. I wanted to prompt him, but just from the way he'd behaved in the diner and his silence on the walk home was enough for me to know that he'd tell me in his own good time. He looked right passed me as he spoke. It was if I wasn't there, yet I knew that he felt he had to tell someone. I followed his gaze through the window, across the field to the distant line of trees along the railroad.

'We went for a walk,' he said suddenly. 'After the game. We won. I felt good. Betty was there, holding up my hand, so proud. She wouldn't let go of me. She was rubbing herself against me, rubbing my chest, my thighs, squeezing my butt. I felt everyone would see, except they didn't, they were far too interested in their own conversations and celebrations. They didn't even notice when Betty pulled me away and led me down towards the creek. She held me close as we walked, nuzzling me, stroking me the whole time. She was making me hot.

'I was tired. I felt good though, buzzing, on a high, after the game. I was still sweating too. The showers had been real hot. We'd walked a mile or more. There was no one about. We went down the bank. She fell on me as I sat down, pushing me back against the sand. She started kissing me, opening my shirt. I tried fondling her, but my heart wasn't in it, Andrew, but she didn't stop. I ran my hand up her skirt. She was damp. She let me finger her. She pulled down my pants. I was hard. I turned and tried to pull her skirt up. "No," she hissed, "not that. Not today." She kept playing with me, kissing me. I tried to respond, but somehow nothing happened, Andrew. I couldn't concentrate. I knew I didn't want her. I didn't want to be there. I could feel myself getting softer, despite her attention. I didn't know where I wanted to be.

'Then, suddenly, it was over. Betty stood, pushed down her skirt, brushed herself and looked down at me. It was awful, Luke. She was condescending, arrogant, angry, and hurt. Her pride was hurt. I don't think she could understand how a guy wouldn't, couldn't, respond to her and her attentions, her passion. She turned, you know how girls do, and stamped away, like a small, spoiled child, told she couldn't have any candy.

I felt for him. I didn't think Betty would say anything though, even to her coterie of girlfriends, it would be too humiliating for her. They're probably hear exactly the opposite, how successful and satisfying the encounter had been.

Rob was nearly crying then.

'I don't know what's wrong with me, Andrew,' he sobbed. 'We've done it before, well not quite everything, but, you know,' he added, suddenly embarrassed, perhaps more by the words than the thought of the actions, 'but I got off. She got me off. I had my eyes closed. I didn't have problems then.'

I moved across to where he was lying, on my bad, and sat down beside him. I put my hand on his thigh. I'd meant it as a friendly gesture, genuinely, not a pass or anything sexual. I'd hardly been there a second when he leaned forward and hugged me, crying loudly into my shoulder.

I was shocked. No one, not least another guy, had ever done this to me. I wondered what was happening. I hadn't really started to think when Rob started caressing me, feeling my body, my sides, my thighs.

'Rob,' I said, panting, 'stop, please, what is going on?'

He pulled my hand from his thigh. He pulled it towards his groin. I could feel his cock. It was huge. It was hard, so, so, so hard.

'That's what's going on, Luke,' he said, leaning back and at last looking me directly in the eyes. 'You're having that effect on me.'

I tried to pull myself back, but he was holding me too tightly.

'You're a guy, Luke, you know what a guy needs.'

I couldn't deny it.

… and Dad and Rob

It hadn't taken long, continued Luke. Suddenly, I'd replaced Betty in every possible way. I was in Rob's thoughts, not her. I pulled down his pants. I'd hardly touched his cock when he shot. It took me longer to find a towel and wipe him clean. He cried then, but the tears were different. They were tears of relief, of self-discovery. We'd hugged.

I'd been in bed reading when Dad finally came home that night.

I'd forgotten the beers. Dad noticed the empty bottles.

'Company?' he asked.

'Yes,' I said, I had nothing, well almost nothing to hide. 'Rob from the football team, you know, the captain. He came into the diner. We walked home together. It seemed friendly, Dad. He'd had a hard day.'

My Dad had smiled.

'That's nice, son,' he said.

After that Rob would call by quite often. We had a secret, our secret. He knew I liked other guys and I knew that he did. He'd come on his bicycle, usually after a practice session. He'd be hot and horny. Usually, we'd stand, pants down, shirts up, hugging as we jerked each other off. It was fairly crude and basic, but it was what we both needed.

That's what we were doing the day Dad saw us. Well, it was how it had started at least. We'd moved on over the months. We'd started sucking each other, getting to know each other's bodies better. It had become a little strained, we both wanted to be on our knees in front of the other. I wanted to be worshipping Rob's sportsman's body, licking it as it got bigger and firmer. For Rob, there was something about giving up his role of hero and icon. For some dumb reason, the idea of sixty-nine-ing hadn't occurred to us.

Dad broke the ice that evening.

'Rob's wonderful, isn't he?' he said, almost nonchalantly as he cooked dinner for himself.

'Sure,' I said.

I didn't think anything of the remark at first. Dad had seen Rob's bike outside often enough. He knew we'd become friends, but I didn't think he knew all the circumstances.

It wasn't until Dad caught my eye that it fell into place. I'm not sure whether it was the full horror of it or the full implications. I thought it was horror for a moment at first. There was a glint in his eye.

'He sure has a great body,' Dad said, 'and a great cock.'

I was about to go bashful, but there was something in his expression. He wasn't admonishing me. He wasn't correcting me, or being disapproving. I was confused. He smiled again.

'I hope you're enjoying it,' he said.

I had to sit down. My mind was spinning. I put my head in my hands.

'Dad?' I asked, 'am I hearing you correctly?'

He turned from the range, putting down the skillet.

He was grinning.

'I sure hope you are,' he said.

I was confused.

'You know about me and Rob?' I said. I wanted to be sure.

'Yes,' Dad said. 'I know now. I saw you.'

I went red.

'This afternoon.'

I started to get up.

I was even more confused.

'And?' I said, confronting him.

'And what?' he said.

'I don't know,' I answered, sitting back down again, suddenly.

'You're my Dad,' I said, 'aren't you supposed to be horrified? Disapproving? Aren't you supposed to beat me? Throw me out?'

'Why should I do that, son?' he said, leaving the range and coming towards me. He bent over the chair, put his arms round me, placed his head next to mine and kissed me. 'Why should I do that?'

He left the question hanging. I reached up and held one of his hands. I was starting to cry. I felt closer to him than I had in a long time. I didn't know why. I could feel him breathing more deeply too.

I watched as he went back to the range and put a bowl into the oven. He pulled two beers from the icebox and handed me one.

He sat down opposite me.

I was uncomfortable. I still wasn't sure. I knew he was going to say something. I thought it was about me. I certainly wasn't prepared for what was coming. Now, though, I think perhaps I should have been. There had been enough clues over the years. It was probably that I was young, genuinely naive and innocent. I hadn't recognized the signs; I hadn't seen them.

He took a sip of beer then reached for my hand.

'Luke, son,' he said, uneasily, 'I think I'm actually pleased I saw what I did this afternoon.'

I was startled.

What? I thought. I shook my head. I thought my ears were deceiving me.

'I think it will make it easier for you to understand,' Dad said. He paused. 'It's why Mom left.'

I looked at him. I wasn't sure that I understood what he was trying to say. I'd been too young to have sex when Mom had walked out. Had Dad been playing with me? I didn't remember that. Mom had been strict, but I hadn't been abused as a child. He saw my confusion.

'I should explain a little more,' he said. 'I was doing what you were doing this afternoon,' he said.

His meaning became clearer. I must have looked surprised though.

'With your Uncle Kent,' he added, before I'd had time to ask.

'I loved your Mom, Luke, I sure did, but I liked men more, well, for sex that is, and your Mom, well, I don't know how much you remember, but, well,' he paused for a while, sipping some beer, 'she wasn't really that sexual a person, not back in those days.' I looked at him. I was only eighteen. It wasn't that long ago.

'And me?' I asked.

If sex wasn't that important, how come I was there? I needed to know.

Dad smiled and squeezed my hand. He read my mind.

'You were deliberate, Luke. We wanted you. We wanted to do the right thing, we wanted to be a nice family, with two kids and a car, perhaps even a dog. It was planned. There'd be you, and then about a year later, we'd try for a brother or sister.

'It took time. People talked, not about Mom and I having sex, but because they knew we were trying for a family, as people say. Then, suddenly, there she was, pregnant. We tried again after you were born. We didn't make love. The sex was mechanical. We were trying to make a baby. We were making it hell for ourselves. Mom wanted the baby but she didn't want sex. I don't think she really wanted me then. It was in the dark. She wouldn't even undress for me before the lights went out and the drapes were closed real tight. She started going to the doctors. They had no answers. I went too. There was nothing physically wrong, they said, with either of us, but still, no conception; no baby. After a while, your Mom stopped trying. I'd make a suggestion, a roundabout remark, something simple, like "tonight?" before going to bed. "No," she'd say, shaking her head. After a while, I stopped even asking. Often, I'd sleep in the spare bed in your room. Sometimes, I could hear her crying, alone, as she tried to sleep.

'It's strange. You know that old expression about what goes around comes around?' Dad asked.

We were still holding hands.

'Kent had been a pal in school, a bit like you and Rob, I suppose. He'd gone into the military from school, never married. Sure people had asked questions, but the answers had always been the same; he was more interested in his career than a family; the time wasn't right; he hadn't met the right girl; he was always on the move, around the world, from base to base. I knew. I knew alright. Billy wasn't the marrying kind.'

Dad smiled. I did too. I knew exactly what he meant. I could remember Uncle Kent, just. I'd remember him coming to the house in his fatigues, his broad chest showing off proudly under a tight tee-shirt, the pants tucked into his boots.

'Kent had come to visit,' Dad said. I could see tears in his eyes. I wasn't sure whether it was reliving the pain or lost love. 'Mom was out. She'd taken you somewhere. I can't remember where, it doesn't matter. I'd had Kent's cock in my mouth when she came home and found us. Kent fled as soon as she appeared. He zipped himself up and was gone. That was the last time I saw him. Mom, well, she ranted and she raved, she smashed crockery, she swore. She packed her bags and she left. I gave her all the cash I had that afternoon.

She put on her Sunday hat, called a cab and went to the airport. That was the last time I saw her too. I lost the two of the three most significant people in my life that afternoon, Luke.

I held both my father's hands then. The tears were running down his face. So many questions, including lots I hadn't even thought of, had been answered. So much was explained. He looked up at me.

'But, I still have you, son,' he said, 'and I have my honesty.'

I was crying to by then.

Dad pulled back a hand and wiped his eyes.

'I can't stop you being you, son,' he said. 'The last thing you should ever be is dishonest, to anyone, least of all yourself.

He took another deep breath.

'Look, son,' he said. 'Your Dad's a cocksucker, but that doesn't make him a bad person.'

He paused, trying to work out what to say next.

I hurried to get there first.

'Look, Dad,' I said, trying to be brave, to "be a man", 'you're son's a cocksucker too.'

The word felt difficult to say, especially that first time.

'... And he's not going to love anyone any less, or think badly of them, or criticize any one else who is, least of all if they're his Dad.'

'There's nothing to be ashamed of, son, not in loving another man. Let nobody tell you that there ever is. Sure, some of them preacher folk, them priests, will try, but me, I think they're just riddled with guilt. They protest too much. They probably had a great time, just like you, in their teens, but they've had no one to talk to about it. All they've had is others saying it's bad. So, what do they do? They get even more uptight. They try to assuage what they see as guilt by blaming others. That's not right, Luke.'

Dad was letting off some steam now.

'If they could find another blow job that was as memorable as that adolescent highpoint, they'd be happy. But, oh no, they can't do that. They can't be honest with themselves. You don't have to be gay, Luke, to appreciate another man's hand, or his mouth, or his ass. It helps, sure, but ask any guy who served in the military, when needs must, you get the most pleasure from what's available. Some of those guys can't even jerk-off without going to confession. Take my word for it.'

Dad turned away after that. I said nothing. I just watched as he turned back to cooking his meal.

The rest of that evening was unusually calm. After Dad had eaten, we sat together, side-by-side on the deck, holding hands. We shared beers. We didn't need to say any more. We were tired. The emotion had drained us both.

Life changed after that. Our lives became even closer. Dad would come by school to meet me after class when he could. Some of the other guys thought it unusual. I loved the affection and joy we found in each other. Dad was even home the next time Rob called by. He smiled, a knowing, almost envious smile, when we went upstairs. That afternoon was a powerful one too. I'd thought about it long and hard. I'd learned by then, and I planned what I wanted to say and how. I started by reminding Rob of my pledge of honesty to him, when he'd first told me about Betty and his feelings. I asked him for a similar promise. When I got it, I told him about Dad. I told him then that Dad also knew all about us.

'He doesn't disapprove?' Rob had asked, astounded.

'No,' I said.

'If he feels we know what we are doing, that we're happy inside, then he's okay. But, he did say we have to be real careful. The law, Rob, doesn't think we're old enough to know our own minds. We can drive, but we can't have sex with one another. We certainly shouldn't try to have sex with older guys, we could get them into real trouble.

'He doesn't look like a faggot, your Dad,' Rob said. He paused. 'But then, you don't either. I didn't think I did. I see these guys on TV, in the papers, they're so camp, effeminate. I'm not like that, Luke, I like men.'

I smiled. I liked men too. I knew what he meant. There was a gleam in his eye. I could see him thinking, but I wasn't sure what was going on inside his mind.

We didn't have sex that day. We'd hugged, sure we had.

'Your Dad, eh, Andrew, who'd have thought it?' said Rob.

I'd smiled. I knew some of our contemporaries had had adolescent crushes on some of the younger mothers; we'd written that off to teenage lust, nothing more, nothing less, but their gossip, their speculation about who might, or might not, be the best neighbor to have as a Mrs Robinson didn't interest us.

'So,' I teased Rob, 'you've got the hots for my Dad then?'

He smiled and held my hand.

'Would I tell you if I did? he said, not answering my question.

He stayed for dinner and a couple of beers that evening.

We talked, or rather he got Dad talking. I sure felt relaxed as we sat, having eaten, lazing around in shorts.

When, finally, Rob left, we cleared the beers away and made our way to the stairs, it was Dad who spoke first. He reached for me and hugged me as he did.

'That sure was a beautiful compliment, Luke, but I am going to have to be careful, very careful.'

I looked at him, not fully understanding.

'Your friend Rob, coming on to me like that.'

He smiled.

'He's a nice kid, a nice guy, but he's still young, too young.'

Dad looked at me, as if wanting help. I shrugged. I didn't know what I could say.

'Look' Dad said, 'if he says anything, if you want to say anything, I suppose it has to be that he can look, but he can't touch, at least not for a couple of years.'

He grinned.

'Is that okay?'

I smiled then.

'Yeah,' I said, 'that's okay. It feels awkward, though,' I said. 'I want him to fancy me, but I'm flattered he has the hots for you, my Dad,' I said, squeezing his arm.

I got word to Rob the next day. I felt I should tell him as soon as I could, before he got too passionate. I knew he wasn't likely to do anything stupid, but people do strange things when they fall in lust. I told him upfront as we walked away from the school that afternoon. He hadn't been upset, I was pleased about that. He said he'd appreciated the honesty.

He hadn't been intending to come into the house that afternoon. We'd parted outside my house, but as soon as I'd gone in, I'd found the brochure and the note.

I'd run outside and called him back.

The brochure was a promotion for the facility where Dad worked. There was one photo of Dad on the front page, clean, neat and respectable in a shirt and tie, introducing him as the manager. Inside, as part of a feature on a sponsored swim for charity, there was a second picture, of him wearing striped Speedos beside the pool. I saw Rob's eyes light up. I smiled and waved a finger at him, teasing rather than reprimanding. He grinned.

'The note is important, Rob,' I said, trying to draw his attention away from the picture. Rob seemed more interested in Dad in his Speedos.

'The facility needs a new assistant Rob,' I stressed, 'to cover a range of duties at weekends, and a help-wanted advert will be running in the local paper this week. If you want the job, call Dad's deputy now,' I said. 'Go by there. Ask for the job'.

I pointed to the phone.

* * *

Dad was smiling when he came home.

'Yes?' I asked.

'It was a no-brainer,' said Dad. 'He was hired within about five minutes. The résumé is impressive, he looks good, he knows how to flatter the ladies, and, what's even better, I know, even though no one else does, that we're not going to have any problems if they pay him too much attention.'

I shook my head, laughing at the irony of it all.

'Has another young deputy coach been providing one of the lady members with too personal a service?' I asked, a penny finally dropping.

'You got it, Luke,' Dad said, "We fired the guy two days ago.'

* * *

Rob's time at the sports faculty worked out well for everyone. He was allowed to use the gym there and got a staff discount on supplements. Without the distractions and interruptions he got at school, his body became even more impressive.

No one thought anything of the time he spent with Dad. It made sense for Rob to ride with him to work, especially in the winter.

When the spring came, they started running. When Dad and Mr Ortiz, the coach at school, had met and agreed that Rob really did have the potential for college football, no one minded at all that he spent more time with us than at home. His mother certainly didn't mind. She could happily get on with playing bridge and drinking gin while we thought about diet and exercise.

Dad became more strict with Rob. If he was going to go for the big time, he said, he had to have the discipline, be able to maintain the pace. He had to have the stamina, the endurance and the control. I got drawn into it too. I had little choice. If I wanted to eat, I ate what they ate, when they ate. If I wanted to talk to Dad, spend time with him, I exercised with him or ran with him. I didn't mind it in the least. I started to feel better, look better as a result. I liked how I looked in the mirror.

The discipline increased. Dad and Mr Ortiz calculated how many calories Rob should eat, what the food groups should be, and how much exercise he should do every day. I was worried, but Rob seemed to be enjoying it. He told me he loved the attention. He loved the look he was creating. He loved the feelings he got from his body when he'd been working it hard. I wasn't sure, but I felt Dad knew what he was doing. He'd dismissed my questions. Rob's okay, he'd say. He's growing. Haven't you seen, he'd ask, how the tougher it gets, the more he does? There was something going on that I didn't fully understand.

There were some fun times, too. That last summer, before

we graduated, Rob finally got his college football offer. The local TV station and newspaper wanted to talk to him, take pictures.

Dad set it up so the only place they could do it was in the pool.

'You want to look your best, don't you, Rob,' Dad had asked, a day or so before.

Rob hadn't said anything. He'd merely grinned.

He'd been sitting on the deck, waiting for dinner. A protein drink had replaced the beers.

Rob had leisurely been adding sets of crunches, fifty at a time, to his already demanding routine as he'd waited for the school to say yes. He did look good, I thought as I watched the grill.

I hadn't been paying too much attention to where Dad had gone until I heard the whirring. I was puzzled. I went through to the living room. Dad had turned off the hair clippers and was covering some of the floor with newspapers. He called Rob in. I hadn't noticed the Speedos on the back of the chair until then. They were the striped pair Dad had been wearing in the brochure picture.

'Try these,' he said, handing them to Rob.

The younger man looked hesitant.

'Now,' Dad said firmly.

Rob obeyed. I watched, trying to disguise my curiosity as much as I could, as he pulled down the baggier workout shorts he'd been wearing. He left his jockstrap in place as he folded the shorts and put them neatly on a chair. I could see that his cock was hardening as he pulled the jock down and put it on top of the shorts.

Dad shook his head as Rob tried to point his hardening cock downwards into the swimbriefs.

'Upwards,' Dad said.

Rob could just do that.

He looked great, I had to admit.

Dad steered him to where he could see himself in the full length mirror on the hall closet door. Rob fought to catch his breath.

'Wow,' he said, 'they look as good as they feel.'

The stripes described the contents of the briefs spectacularly. Rob moved round so he could see the curves of his butt too. I was impressed. I knew what Dad had in mind. I couldn't wait to see how Rob would look on TV and in the paper.

'You could look even better, you know Rob,' Dad said, standing discretely beside him.

'Yeah?' Rob said, his breathing hot and horny.

Dad ran his hand through the sumptuous forest of hair across Rob's chest and the pattern that ran down his stomach.

'You've worked so hard, Rob,' Dad said, 'that it seems a shame no one can see those pecs, or,' he ran his hand down the young man's body, 'these abs.'

I smiled.

At that moment, I realized why the clippers were there.

Dad picked them up and flicked the switch. He looked at Rob. He wanted the young man's approval. There was no denying Rob was excited at his own appearance. He rubbed the hair. Dad turned his head to one side.

He was waiting.

The young man looked in the mirror again.

'It'll grow back,' Dad said.

I could see Rob's brain at work. He was tempted, sorely tempted. He was proud of the fur. It made him feel more manly, more adult, I remembered him saying. But Dad's appeal to his vanity had hit home. I noticed the moment when it won.

'Okay,' he said to Dad a moment later, 'go for it.'

Dad guided him on to the newspaper. He put the young man's hands behind his back and nudged his feet apart with his boot. Rob closed his eyes and bowed his head. It was a magnificent sight. Dad took the clippers very carefully to the flesh. He wasn't intending to mark it at all.

'Not a movement, Rob, not a fraction,' he said, quietly. I could just see the brief nod of Rob's acknowledgment.

I stood there watching as the thick dark pelt fell to the floor. I watched as Dad carefully, precisely took the clippers round each nipple. I heard Rob's intake of breath and I noticed the twitch inside the Speedos as Dad held each nipple, guiding the teeth of the clippers to the nearest hairs. I watched as he worked exactly into the cleavage between Rob's pectoral muscles, down his front. I could see first a two-pack, then four, then the six as the hair fell away. I saw Rob trying not to move as the clippers tickled him as they cleared hair from his belly button. I was sure Dad was teasing him by running his little finger into the opening to brush away the clippings. It must have tickled, but Rob wasn't giving in. He was determined. I watched as he ran the clippers towards the waistband of the briefs. He didn't stop there. He walked round Rob and pushed his hands to the front. I could see Rob wanting to touch himself, to feel the new clear, clean skin, but he didn't. He put his hands in front of his waist, keeping them away even from his cock, while Dad took the clippers to the hair on his shoulders and back.

Dad had been right. The hair did hide so much more of Rob's beauty. The definition was so much clearer without the darkness to hide it. I had to smile. I hadn't appreciated that even when he reached the briefs at the back, he hadn't finished with Rob.

Dad brushed the worst of the clippings off him with his

hand, almost slapping his belly and shoulders. I could see Rob smile. He was sure then that he was being teased, but he kept his eyes firmly shut. I could see the piles of hair on the newspaper on the floor. I wondered if he knew there'd be so much.

I watched as Dad maneuvered Rob back to the position in front of the mirror. He pulled Rob's hands and arms back behind him.

'Okay,' he said at last, 'you can look.'

I remember vividly the look of joy and amazement that slowly spread across Rob's face as he saw his new image. His eyes were wide and the grin grew slowly but steadily. No words came out, but his lips described the loudest 'wow' the house had ever heard. I could see him straining, holding his hands behind his back.

'Yes,' Dad said, reading the signs.

Rob felt himself gently at first, tracing his fingertips across his hard flesh. It was hard to avoid the cock twitching in the briefs. Dad didn't let him have long. He pulled the hands back. He stood in front of Rob and started blowing gently on the naked skin.

I could see Rob's fingers open. Even though his eyes were closed again, his eyebrows were rising towards his hairline. I saw him shake his head and catch his breath.

'Yes?' Dad said, as he bent and blew into Rob's belly button.

I was amazed when Rob simply bent forward and gently kissed Dad on his head. It was a gesture that meant so much.

'It's not quite finished,' Dad said. 'You'll have to trim it with a razor in the shower, but be careful. And remember to use plenty of calamine lotion afterwards,' he smiled. 'It prevents a lot of problems. You don't want razor rash now, do you?'

Rob nodded.

'And there's another thing,' he said.

Rob looked puzzled, the expression of delight vanishing from his face in an instant.

'Yes?' said Rob, tremulously.

'Here,' Dad said, pulling the hair at the top of Rob's Speedos, 'and here', as he pulled the pubic hair from the side. Rob looked chastened.

Again, I could see Dad's expression; he was forthright, demanding.

'There's no point in doing half a job, is there, Rob?'

There was no hesitation this time.

'Go for it, Sir,' he said. It was the first time I'd heard him call Dad anything but Mr Pulaski.

Rob quickly closed his eyes, put his hands behind his back and bowed his head.

It was an impressive sight.

Dad loosened the cord in the Speedos and pushed them down Rob's thighs. His cock bounced obediently to attention. I was thick and veined, I knew. I smiled as Dad held it, almost clinically and pushed it down out of the way as he took the clippers carefully to more of Rob's hair. He worked determinedly but attentively. It didn't take long for all the hair above Rob's cock and balls to hit the floor. I could see the delicious range of expressions crossing Rob's face as Dad kept the cock behind his wrist as he handled the balls, guiding the whirring teeth across the sensitive and delicate skin. Rob grimaced as Dad bent forward to blow the clippings away. A dribble had appeared at Rob's pisshole.

Rob kept his eyes closed as Dad steered him again towards the mirror. The Speedos around his thighs made movement more difficult. Rob's cock was still rock hard, sticking out in front of his body. I wondered if Dad would use it as he had before, as a handle. I suddenly realized just how much this little ceremony was turning me on. I hadn't appreciated until that moment just how hard my own cock was. I found I had put my own hands behind my back. At that moment, I was jealous, very jealous, of Rob. I wanted to be there, for someone to be holding me, shaving me, someone for whom I could bow my head. It didn't matter that it was Dad. That it was a someone who was slightly older, but in very good shape helped. I tried to take deep breaths.

I moved forward as Dad placed Rob in front of the mirror.

'Open your eyes,' he said again.

Rob obeyed.

I could see the shock. His eyes were motionless for a split second, then they sprang open, his eyebrows shooting upwards. His mouth fell open. He shook his head.

Dad was smiling too.

'Isn't that better, Rob?' he said. 'You can see so much more. That cock looks bigger than ever.'

Even Rob smiled now. He seemed to want to pull his hands from behind his back, as if afraid that he shouldn't do so without permission.

Dad noticed.

'Yes,' he said, 'go on, touch yourself, feel how much more beautiful you are to touch, Rob.'

The hands came round slowly. Rob almost seemed scared of how he would feel.

His hands went to his stomach first. He took a short but deep intake of breath as his fingers met the flesh. There was an expression of incredulity across his face. He was watching himself in the mirror. Dad had moved back, standing a few inches away from him. Rob looked as if he was seeing someone entirely new in the mirror.

'Don't you like that, Rob?' Dad asked. 'Don't you feel like

you have been born anew? That you're a new person? Leaving the old Rob, the child, behind?'

I smiled.

Rob was still tingling as he ran a single finger from his abdominals down towards his cock and balls. The expression on his face had not changed. He was moving his back and shoulders as the sensations ran up his spine for the first time. I had no doubt it would not be the last.

My attention was so focused on Rob that I hadn't noticed that Dad had disappeared. I was wanting to be there too, sharing the moment.

Rob noticed me at last. He beckoned that I should go to him. He smiled at me. As soon as I was near enough, he bent forward and kissed me. He took my hand and ran it down his flesh. It felt awesome, better than I'd ever known it. There was still some stubble, waiting for the finality of a razor.

'You should try it, Luke,' Rob said at last. 'It's so good.'

I wondered if I was really ready.

'Perhaps you should.' Dad was back. I hadn't noticed him.

'Why don't you, Luke?' said Dad. 'You'd look so good alongside Rob.'

The decision and the words had hit me like a spell. I was entranced. I could hardly move. It was like hypnosis. I was aware that Dad had pulled my tee-shirt from my cut-offs and was pulling it up over my head. I could feel him undoing the fly of the torn denim, but I did nothing. It felt like someone else. The cut-offs hit the floor. My jockstrap followed. I could feel my cock filling as Dad pulled the supporter down my thighs.

He turned me round, on to the newspaper before starting the clippers. I didn't have as much hair as Rob. When testosterone had hit him, the forest had sprung to life. When it hit me, it had taken nearly all my teen years for a few wisps to develop to a noticeable pattern across my stomach and a ring around each nipple. I didn't feel I'd be sorry to lose either.

Without thinking, I put my hands behind my back and closed my eyes as Dad brought the clippers towards me. I tried not to flinch as they touched me for that very first time. The sensation was hard to describe. The skin felt cool, like the breeze when you get to the beach and take your shirt off. It felt very, very sensitive, as if the nerve endings had suddenly had a power boost.

I had to try hard not to laugh or to come as Dad ran the clippers round my cock and balls. When he held my cock, I wanted to lean forward, put my head on his shoulders and cry. I wanted to hug him, but I held my hands firmly behind my back, the fingers of one hand digging into the wrist of the other.

I didn't look either until Dad had steered me in front of the mirror.

My jaw dropped then. I hadn't appreciated just how much definition I had in my abs. My cock was upright and proud too. I'd never seen myself like that. It was like looking at a guy posing in a magazine, only that guy was alive and that guy was me. It was difficult to think. My brain was being overloaded with the physical sensation of the air against my newly-released skin. My eyes were aghast at the eroticism of the image in front of me. Deep in my psyche, some thing was happening too. I could feel my knees giving way. I was kneeling. I wanted to give this image, to develop, maintain it, I wanted to serve. Without warning, the tears exploded.

Then, they were there. Rob was kneeling too. He placed himself at one side of me, a knee between my legs, supporting me with his broad chest. Dad was at the other side, standing, so I could rest my head on his thigh. I felt the slight roughness of his jeans on my cheek as my tears dampened the denim. I felt Rob reach behind me and hold my hands in place. I turned from Dad and kissed him; we both knew exactly what was happening for each other.

Dad moved away then. He stood and watched as Rob and I rested on one another. We both had our hands behind our backs. I could feel the musculature of Rob's chest moving rhythmically up and down, in and out, as he fought to keep his breathing under control. We held our cheeks together, feeling the warmth and security of the other.

Dad pulled Rob up first.

I opened my eyes when the heat of his naked flesh disappeared. Dad had moved fast, making the most of the opportunity. There was a bowl steaming on the table. I watched as Dad removed a cloth and rubbed hot water onto Rob's bare skin. I saw how Rob flinched for a second in response to the heat. Dad rubbed the skin hard, softening the bristle. He covered Rob with foam, his balls disappearing beneath the white lather, his cock hardening more. It took Dad a while. He worked carefully and slowly.

Rob communicated every reaction with his face. One moment he was scared, worried that the blade might cut him, then he was smiling, transmitting the beauty of the sensation. Throughout, his cock never once became any softer. It jerked; he did too, when Dad pulled his ballsac for the first time, running the blade across the taut skin in long, straight strokes.

Eventually, Dad seemed satisfied.

'Go shower,' he said, almost clinically, to Rob.

I waited. I was alone for a few minutes. Dad had taken the bowl to the kitchen. When he came back, it was steaming again. He guided me by my shoulders as I stood up again. He looked at me straight in the eyes. I looked at him too. I compared our two bodies, the father and the son. He was taller, not much, probably no more than an inch or so, perhaps two, about six foot. He was thicker set. I wondered how much had come from working out. He was in good shape. His chest was strong, waist narrow, butt still pert and, so far, his hips were trim too. I hoped I could stay so fit so long. Even in his check shirt, jeans and boots he looked good. He felt good too.

Even though it was probably only a few seconds, it felt ages before he stood back and started rubbing my skin with the hot cloth.

I flinched too.

Dad looked at me, reprovingly.

'I'm sorry,' formed on my lips, although no sound emerged. He knelt this time, working equally slowly and carefully as he had with Rob. I tried not to look. I wanted to feel. My eyes closed and my hands went behind my back. It was hard keeping my knees from giving way.

I wanted that to last for ever. The situation, my supplication, the sensations; I had never known anything which seemed so perfect, so ideal. I had no idea where I was when I felt the cloth washing away the last of the foam.

'You should shower too,' Dad said. It wasn't quite as direct an order as he'd given Rob, but it was certainly an instruction. I thought I should have been embarrassed as I set off up the stairs, my erection bouncing in front of me. Instead, there was a feeling of pride, of fulfillment.

Rob was drying himself down when I reached the bathroom. There was no denying that losing the body hair had dramatically increased his impressiveness. I was old enough then to know that for some guys, body hair is important. I wasn't among them. The firmness and the definition of the muscle meant more to me. If I could see it, better still, if I could feel it, that was my desire.

I knew, somewhere deep inside, that I shouldn't really have done it, but I went up to Rob. I stood directly in front of him and rubbed my hands from his neck to his balls. It was a hard motion at first. Then, I caressed him. I gently ran my fingers from the sides of his ears, around his chin and down his neck, across his shoulders and under the curve of each pec. I tickled each of the newly-revealed abdominal muscles. I teased a finger into the crease between each leg and a fingertip back behind his ball sac. My cock grew harder when I heard him draw breath, sharply, through clenched teeth. I bent then, and quickly, but genuinely, kissed the head of his cock.

I said nothing as I went into the shower and washed off the last of the drying lather. I ran my hands repeatedly across my own freed stomach and around my balls. I was so hard, yet I didn't touch my cock. There was something within me that said I shouldn't. I didn't.

Rob was standing in the kitchen doorway when I got back downstairs. I could see the striped Speedos emphasizing the curves of his butt. He was talking to Dad.

Dad smiled when I appeared.

'On the table, Luke, behind you,' he said, 'there's something for you.'

I wondered what it was as I turned.

The package was small, three or four inches square. The blue paper was neatly sealed. I pulled it open gently. My mouth fell open with glee when I saw what was inside – another pair of the striped Speedos.

I heard Dad's voice from behind me.

'Put them on.'

This time it really was an order.

I obeyed.

The Speedos felt so good. I had to fight to keep my cock inside them, it was so hard. Rob and I looked at one another, the smiles rampant across our faces.

'This way.'

It was another order from Dad.

We both turned. Neither of us expected the sharp instant of light as the flashgun fired in.

It caught us by surprise.

I was about to become indignant, petulant, when Rob caught me. He was laughing. I didn't know how he could. The pictures would be so humiliating, I thought. Rob grasped my shoulders as Dad fired off another shot.

'Don't you see, Luke?' Rob asked.

I shook my head.

There was a third flash, then more, as Rob moved us both around.

'You'll know soon enough,' he said, moving me again.'

The reveal

Rob and I kept the Speedos on when Dad finished taking the pictures. It had taken me a little while to appreciate what he'd been looking for. Another dimension would have been added to the shots of two good bodies by the matching Speedos.

The proof of Dad's thinking came when Rob appeared on TV and in the newspaper. He looked amazing. He'd looked so hot. Although I had nothing really to do with what was going on, I made sure I just happened to be there. Okay, I admitted later to Dad, I was just as star-struck as anyone.

It had been an interesting afternoon. The school principal had been full of pomposity. He'd talked about honor and determination. He'd filled his chest so full he couldn't look down. He'd spoken, said too much, and then left. It was as if he felt he had to look far busier and far more important than he really was.

Rob was great, genuine and honest. The TV station had sent Marie-Helene. She was young, straight out of college into her first on-screen job. She was very blonde and looked as if she'd spent every spare penny on having her teeth fixed and whitened. Within days of her first appearance on air, ratings for the station's news shows among young males had rocketed. Of course, she'd said to the local newspaper, she'd got the job on ability, not looks.

Marie-Helene was no stooge. She knew a prime ability was to flash her smile and win over viewers. She was also learning fast how to turn any assignment to her own advantage.

I made sure that I'd been gently swimming lengths of the pool when Marie-Helene and her cameraman arrived. I recognized her, but he got more of my attention. He was broad shouldered, had a crew cut and a tight butt. I liked what I saw. I got out and walked towards him as Marie-Helene, Dad and Rob talked about what was going to happen.

'Hi,' the cameraman spoke as I approached. His greeting surprised me.

'Hi,' I said.

'I'm Ryan, Ryan Cameron, pleased to meet you,' he said, holding out his hand and looking me down and up, carefully as he did so.

I smiled, flattered, his interest more than obvious.

'He's a good-looking guy,' Ryan said, looking towards Rob.

'He sure is,' I added, not sure whether I should say any more.

'Is there anywhere I can change?' Ryan asked. His question puzzled me.

'Sure,' I said. I thought quickly. 'Follow me.'

He did. I led him towards the locker room.

'I want to get some shots from in the pool,' Ryan said. 'I thought it would look good to see him diving in, only from underneath.'

I smiled.

'I'm sure that would look great, quite an image,' I said, turning to see a broad grin across Ryan's face. I knew instantly that it wasn't just the drama of the shot that was boosting his creativity.

I waited just to one side as Ryan took off his trainers and socks. I tried to be as nonchalant as I could as he pulled a pair of Speedos from his pocket. It was hard not to smile when he dropped his jeans, leaving a swimmer's narrow-waistband jockstrap plainly in view. I hadn't seen one of those before; I was intrigued.

'Now that,' I said to myself, 'was interesting.'

I tried to work out Ryan's age as he pulled on the Speedos. His butt and thighs were firm. There was a neat tan line too; mid- to late-twentiess, I reckoned as he hung up the jeans and turned back towards me.

'"You busy?' asked Ryan as I led him back towards the pool, my attention fixed on the bit of jockstrap that was just visible above the Speedos.

'"No,' I said, 'why?'

He pointed towards the camera and some other equipment at the side of the pool.

'Just keep an eye on things,' he said, 'bring me anything I may need.'

He grinned.

'An extra pair of hands can make such a difference,' he said.

The expression was captivating.

I watched as Ryan got into the water, got the video camera onto his shoulder and filmed Rob diving in.

Did it really need five takes, I wondered, as Rob climbed out of the water yet again.

Marie-Helene was certainly making the most of the opportunity. I hadn't noticed that she'd disappeared too while Rob was busy diving.

When she reappeared, she too was in swimwear. Her one-piece costume was a luscious deep yellow, cut low and emphasizing her tan and her ample breasts. With her like that and Rob at his most splendid, that night's show would certainly be hitting the peaks of audience appreciation, I thought, and they're have fun with the trailers, for once genuinely teasing the TV audience.

They set up the first shots of the interview on the steps to the safety chair. Marie-Helene was probably no more than about five-three tall. Rob was close to six foot. By standing on one of the steps to the lifeguard's look-out seat, their heads were level. Ryan scooted round them. He even jumped back into the water and took some shots looking upwards. As I bent to hand him the camera, I turned and caught a glimpse of what the shot would be like. There would be no avoiding the profiles of either Rob's Speedos or Marie-Helene's cleavage. As Ryan climbed into the lifeguard's chair to take some downwards shot, I couldn't help but smile.

They decided to finish with a race; just a length. Ryan decided to shoot it from one side, walking sideways along the poolside to keep up. I was, he said, to hold on to his side and steer him as he did. I nearly failed him. It hadn't taken more than a few paces for my attention to stray onto the contents of Ryan's Speedos rather than the direction in which we were moving. He was nearly over the edge and into the pool before I realized what was happening and pulled him back.

I don't think Rob was swimming his fastest, but he certainly didn't look as if he was out for a stroll. His panting when he reached the end made Marie-Helene's performance all the more impressive. She hadn't been far behind him at all. I'd caught Dad's eye while the race was going on. His expression seemed full of praise for her technique. He was there congratulating her and helping her out of the water almost as soon as she'd touched home.

The TV station had certainly made the most of the material. They'd run the piece as the last item in their 5.30 news show, making the audience wait, having trailed it right from the start. They'd used pictures of Rob and Marie-Helene, naked at the shoulders, saying they'd be 'showing us more' later on. They'd used one of Ryan's shots of Rob diving in too, but only showing his face and chest, nothing more.

When the story finally ran, probably very few people would actually have listened to what Rob had to say. Pictures of Rob diving, this time showing him from head to toes, were cut into the interview, so too were shots looking down on him and Marie-Helene from the chair. After the race, the segment ended with the shot Ryan had taken from the pool, slowly pulling back to show the difference in the heights and how Marie-Helene was standing on the steps. The expressions on the anchors' faces when the tape ended were delicious.

They'd cut the report differently for the late-night show. There were shots of Marie-Helene talking to the camera. Ryan's shot teased the viewers beautifully, stopping just short of her cleavage, but leaving the straps of her swimsuit in sight. The upwards profile shot was used too. No one could have been left in any doubt that Rob was a well-made man, and, that night, Marie-Helene became Dolly Helene; Miss Parton, everyone said the following morning, sure had a rival. The comparison was perhaps a little unfair; cameras may not lie, but lenses can certainly flatter. That particular version of the story ended with shots of Dad helping her out of the water and her back as she walked away towards the locker room. He became a town hero too.

I hadn't understood why, but when I took Ryan back to the locker room and loaned him my towel, he'd asked for our address.

The next day, everyone was talking about the coverage, or, as some said, the lack of it.

There was even more of a crowd to see Rob swim than usual. I felt like a groupie, enjoying the second-hand acclamation. I wouldn't have been surprised if someone had produced an autograph book. I could see the guys in their early teens, boys and girls in their own separate groups. Both were whispering questions to one another. The boys as well as the girls seemed desperate to know if Rob was hung as well as the pictures had made him look. I'd deliberately chosen a darker Speedo for Rob that morning. I smiled. Some of them, most of them, would never know.

Even some of the school staff made an excuse to come by that morning. They all seemed to have questions that needed answering that day, or forms where information was apparently missing or unclear. I did what I could to keep everyone at bay while Rob got on with his exercise.

We found out why Ryan had asked for the address for himself, rather than rely on Marie-Helene's notes. When we got home there was a DVD in the mailbox – with a note: 'I thought you might like this; there are the all the pieces which went out and a copy of everything I shot. Ryan.'

We waited for Dad to come home before we ran the

footage. Rob's immediate reaction had been to put it into the machine there and then. I could see the idea of seeing himself again was already turning him on.

'You must learn to have patience,' I told him strongly, taking the tape away. I was just as keen to see what was there, but felt it would be better to wait.

Dad was pleased we did – and delayed the gratification even longer, making us all wait until after we'd eaten before putting playing the DVD.

Summertime living

Luke didn't need encouraging to continue the story.

That summer was interesting, he said. Effectively, we finished school in June, he explained We'd taken the tests. Many of us had found college places. Others were off to work. Rob had his football scholarship. I was set for the state university. We had some time. Rob wasn't due to report until September first. My life as a freshman was scheduled to start a week later, after Labor Day.

For many, it was a summer of relaxation and leisure. Many of our school friends very quickly made the most of their freedom and liberty, getting up late, spending time sunbathing or swimming in the creek, hanging out at the diner or around the town square. It was that last, that only, time of teenage freedom.

For Rob, there was no break. If anything, the work became even more intense. He moved in with us for those last two months. It was, Dad said, so that he could get used to more discipline to prepare him for the rigors of the college football team boot camp.

I don't think there was any actual contact between Rob and Dad. I don't think that after that first shaving Dad ever touched Rob's cock again. He certainly didn't touch mine. Although there might not have been any contact, there was sex in the air.

Rob certainly got into what was happening. Dad's rules became more and more strict. Rob couldn't be a wimp, he said. He had to toughen up, make sure he had the physical stamina to survive the first intense months of college football training. He had to get used to having no privacy too, Dad said; there wouldn't be any in the dorm.

Some of the instructions Dad issued made sense. Rob was allowed only to wear a jock, Speedos or tight shorts when he was in the house. He was banned from using the furniture, except when we were in the kitchen together, eating; he was to sit on the floor. He was never, Dad said, to close his bedroom door either.

I felt I wanted to do many of these things too. I started wearing only Speedos, a jock or shorts around the house. Sometimes Rob and I would swap, may be once, sometimes two or three times a day. In an evening, if we were talking or watching TV, I too would sit on the floor. If Dad noticed, he certainly didn't say anything.

For Rob, the demands on his body grew too. He'd be training six days a week, running, using the gym, and swimming. I'd run with him, swim with him and do some work at the gym, but nowhere near the number of reps or using the amount of weight that Rob did. The seventh day was for swimming.

Often, Rob would be at home, doing more push-ups or crunches out on the deck, I'd be busy in the kitchen. I think Dad had spoken to Rob's future coach at college. A diet sheet arrived. I was put in charge. I suspect some money may have come too. It was demanding – for Rob and for me, as I prepared his meals.

Although we spent a lot of time on our own, we weren't isolated. We'd see a lot of the other guys. Often, folks would come and watch Rob as he swam. If they were out driving when we were running, they'd pull up alongside and talk to Rob and I as we all went along together. Rob was already more than something of a hero in our small town. His TV appearance and his captaincy of the school football team had made him a local celebrity. The college scholarship had been the frosting on the cake. No one could remember when, or even if, anything like this had happened before. It wasn't just his career that was riding on his determination; it was the hopes of the entire township. Rob was set to prove that it was possible escape from hick obscurity by sheer, physical hard work.

Dad had had several long talks with Rob. Rob knew just how great others' expectations had become. Dad had laid out the odds. Rob could either make it, or he'd never be forgiven. He'd probably never be allowed back into the town again. He'd never be able to hold his head up. So, that summer, we worked, we all worked, to make sure that Rob had everything stacked in his favor.

Then, suddenly, one day at the start of September, he was gone.

There was a small turnout at the local airport to see him go. His own folks were there, of course, and his sister. Dad drove us, Rob sitting quietly in the back. Mr Ortiz was there. We got an angry call from the newspaper the next day. Why hadn't we told them? They'd have come and taken a picture. That was exactly why. We wanted it to be a private time.

Rob didn't take much with him. There was a suit, two pairs of chinos, a shirt for each day of the week, a couple of pairs of jeans. He took his Speedos, including the striped ones, and his jockstraps of course, except one. He'd given me that the night before. It was, he'd said, something I was to remember him by. He took a laptop, a parting gift from his Mom, and that was about it.

I'd thought about wearing the jock that day. I hadn't. I wouldn't. I knew somehow that I'd never wear it. I didn't want to spoil the smell of Rob on it. Instead, I had it in my pocket. I held it tightly as I watched him get into the small commuter plane, as I watched it taxi and take off.

I cooked as usual that night, even though Rob wasn't there. I behaved as usual too. I stripped in the house. I wore only Speedos. I went to sleep with my nose in his jock. I knew I'd miss him.

Rob's hazing

We got the first e-mail the next day, said Luke. It was full of thanks. Sure he was missing us, Rob said, but he was sure prepared for what was happening. The older guys had started the hazing as soon as the youngsters had arrived. There'd been a bus waiting for them all at O'Hare. There were twelve of them in all. Some of the older guys had come out to meet them. They'd started to put us in our places during the three-hour drive out to the training camp, Rob said.

They'd made them strip on the bus, as soon as it had started to get dark, and then had them doing push-ups on the bus floor. They'd had to kiss the older guys' boots each time they went down. One guy had refused and they'd started kicking him. They'd also kicked our balls, Rob said. They were some sure gorgeous guys. It was hot, he'd said, and he'd really had to concentrate to try to keep his dick from getting too hard. Showing that he'd been turned on would have ended his career before it had even started, such was the prejudice then.

Rob hadn't needed any of the gear from home that first day. Everything had been provided – including jockstraps, but it hadn't been until they were starting their workouts that the younger guys had realized that all the pouches had been rubbed with Icy Hot, the medication for sore muscles. The others had been scratching themselves, trying to put out the fire. Rob had just glowed, his cock as hard as a rock. I didn't know what that would be like, so when I'd read what Rob had said, I went to the bathroom and found some. I dropped my Speedos and took some and rubbed it in to my cock and balls. I soon found out. The skin on my sac was still burning when I finally got to sleep.

Dad didn't say anything at first during that last week. He let me go about as I wanted. I'd swim each day and make calls, so everything was ready for me when I left.

I was the one who raised the subject. It was three or four days after Rob had left. We were eating. I wondered how he'd be, on his own. He'd had me around the place for years and more recently Rob too. Suddenly, the house would be empty. He'd be on his own.

'You need company, Dad,' I said, 'someone who can be here, look after you.'

He'd reached for my hand and held it closely. There had been tears in his eyes. His reaction confirmed that I was right.

'Don't you worry, son,' he said, forcing a smile. 'I'll be okay. Trust me.'

I looked at him. I wasn't sure.

'Trust me,' he said again, reading my suspicion.

I nodded, trying to restrain my doubts.

The next day, he took me to college. It was a twelve-hour drive. I drove some. We didn't talk that much. The silence said it all. It was a time of change. It had been some summer;

one of those summers, the sort that happen only once in your teens. Not always the last, but those where there's something you know will never happen again, at least not for you. There was no denying that it had been special. Although we'd come out to each other a while before, we'd been more honest with one another that year. That was so important. Perhaps it was with having had Rob around. I think we'd both found something special in that. I wasn't quite sure what the effect was for me. I thought moving on, going to college, would get me over it.

I'd arranged a room in the dorm. I should have been sharing with two other guys, but one didn't show. It didn't take me long to unpack.

Dad helped.

Although Kyle had arrived, I suddenly felt very alone when I hugged Dad, I even kissed him, looking deep and lovingly into his eyes. He'd tried to avoid my gaze, but gave into me, just for a second. I was still savoring that intimacy as I watched him drive away. There were tears in my eyes. Okay, I could call him, e-mail him every day, perhaps even more than that, but it was different. He wouldn't be so close.

* * *

It's a strange feeling. You can be somewhere where there are lots of people, hundreds, all being very busy, milling around, meeting each other for the first time, but you can still feel alone, very alone, more alone than at any other time. There was also something different about the way Dad and I were together. We were more like friends. The other guys were uneasy, how kids are, as if they're ashamed of what others will think of their folks. I wasn't like that with Dad. I knew him more as a friend than a parent.

May be it was more fraternal. That's what Kyle thought.

'Your brother?' he asked as Dad drove away.

'No,' I answered honestly, sitting down on my bed, 'My Dad.'

'No, really? He's young,' Kyle said.

'He was,' I said. 'He is.' I added, correcting myself.

I smiled, my thoughts following him through town back towards the Interstate.

'He's a hot guy,' I said, without thinking, then suddenly hoping the sentiments weren't inappropriate as far as Kyle was concerned.

I needn't have worried.

'He sure is that,' Kyle said.

'First time?' I looked at him, puzzled.

'You're first time away from home?' he said, clarifying himself.

'For any length of time,' I said.

'No mother?' Kyle asked. He seemed to be reading me very cleverly.

'Not for years,' I said.

'She left us.'

I left it at that.

We sniffed around each other, Kyle and me.

We wondered where our roommate was. No one had told us anything then.

It hadn't taken us long to sort out our things. Kyle was having more shipped from home, he said.

As we hadn't had a chance to meet or get to know anyone else, Kyle and I went out to look for dinner together.

It was when we were eating that the truth started to out. Kyle's pocket book fell open. There was a picture there.

'My turn,' I said, 'brother?'

Kyle was silent for a second too long. He started to say yes, but I could see it wasn't the truth; he wasn't easy with it. I looked at him.

'I was dreading this,' he said, 'especially if I had two roommates.'

I can't say I'm a great believer, but I did offer a short prayer of thanks for the experiences of the previous two years.

'Boyfriend?' I asked.

Kyle looked both surprised and relieved.

'Yes,' he said, looking down, avoiding my eyes.

'What's his name? Been together long?'

Kyle looked up at me. He didn't seem to have been expecting a positive response.

'Michael,' he said. 'A couple of years.'

He paused.

'You don't mind?'

I smiled.

'Not in the least,' I said.

'It makes two of us. Somehow,' I added, pausing for effect, 'I don't think we'll be moving rooms.'

We felt secure in each other's confidence.

If Kyle could come out to me, it was the least I could to reciprocate, to be as honest. It all came tumbling out after that. I told him about Dad, and about Rob, well most of it, but not all, certainly not some of my feelings that summer. He told me about his boyfriend Michael and about his own family. His Dad had been in the military in the Gulf soon after he'd been born. He started getting ill soon after coming home. He'd felt he should stay home and help his mother with the care. He needn't have worried. His father had died a few months earlier.

I liked Kyle, but even though he came from Philadelphia, and had got to know some of the big East Coast cities, I felt that my time with Dad and Rob had given me greater experience, a greater knowledge, certainly greater confidence with my sexuality. Missing Michael, I very soon realized, would be hard for Kyle, very hard.

It was when we got back to the dorm that we met Mr Benini. I still don't know why he came to tell us, not one of the administrators. He'd knocked on our door soon after we'd got back.

He'd got good news, he said. We'd be on our own, for that semester at least, our roommate was a no-show, family illness, he said.

I hardly heard what he was saying I was so taken with him. Even dressed, I could see that Mr Benini had a great body. I could see thighs like tree trunks inside his chinos. His back was a definite V, tapering from broad shoulders. His shirt could hardly contain the biceps pressing against the fabric. A stub of nipple, like a pencil-end eraser, pushed out from his pecs on the right side; I knew there'd be a second, just like it, that was hidden by the shirt pocket on the left. I hadn't realized my mouth was open.

"'Close it, Luke,' Kyle said, as soon as Mr Benini had left, 'you really shouldn't make it so obvious, especially on your very first day.'

"I smiled. And, that, is how I first met Brandon Benini."

Tutor Benini

I got through college motivated by Mr Benini, Luke continued. He taught a class in politics as well as being the college swim team coach. I liked that. I'd never been political, but he inspired me to study. I worked because I hoped it would please him. I worked out too, because I hoped that would also please him. I'd try and get to see him whenever I could. I'd use the gym when I knew he would be there. I would swim when I knew he would be there too. I'd run when I knew he'd be out on the road too.

I got to know that body of his. I'd watch him in shorts as he strained to finish the last bench press. I tried, as nonchalantly as I could to gaze up the legs of those shorts. I'd try not to be too obvious as I waited for him to get out of the pool. He was one of the few staff members who wore Speedos. I never found out whether he wore a jock. I never saw his cock.

Everything changed the day I graduated. Dad had come to campus for the ceremony, but he'd had to go on quickly afterwards; work, he'd said. I was disappointed. I wanted to try to get to know him again. We'd grown apart during my time away. I'd driven him to the airport in a hire car. The plan was that I'd clear my room and then drive home. I was sorry I'd find the family home empty.

Michael was helping Kyle load when I got back.

'Mr Benini said he wanted to see you,' Kyle said, 'as soon as you got here.'

I wondered what he wanted as I walked towards Mr Benini's office. I thought we'd sorted out all the formalities the previous afternoon. I wanted to get packed and hit the road. Dad had given me a little extra cash to pay for a motel so I didn't have to drive the twelve hours without a some rest.

Despite the mixed emotions, the goodbyes, the unknown future, I was ready to make the break.

Mr Benini was sitting on the sofa. He didn't make any effort to get up when he called me in.

'Yes, Coach?' I said, closing the door behind me. It was only when I turned that I appreciated he was wearing only a tanktop and shorts, shorts tighter than those he usually wore in the gym. I tried not to make my gaze too obvious.

'It's no use, Luke,' he said. 'You've made it obvious ever since the very first time we met.'

I was crestfallen. I bowed my head.

'Luke,' he said. 'I have tolerated your playing cocktease for three years. I have said nothing when you've been showing yourself off here on campus or shagging off it.'

The words seemed somehow familiar. So did the setting. I tried to concentrate on what Mr Benini was saying.

'Luke, I am an old-school professor, I have principals. It has been hard, but I haven't touched you, Luke.'

It was my turn to be shocked. Mr Benini notice me? Want to touch me?

'I've tested you Luke, I can't deny that,' he said. 'I brought some of your grades down, not a lot, but enough for you to notice and to try harder. I added to your workout schedules too. But now, Luke, you've graduated. As of an hour ago, you are no longer registered as a student here. You are no longer my pupil. I am no longer your professor. I am a man, Luke, you are another.'

He was staring hard at me now. I could see out of the corners of my eyes. I was so red I could not look at him. He'd known all this time and said nothing.

'You've been looking at me ever since that first day, Luke. You even came to ask me for advice and guidance whenever you could, even when you didn't really need it. You checked whatever you could with me, Luke, don't deny it. I only had to blink and you were there, or you would have been, wouldn't you, Luke?'

He was rubbing it in, but I couldn't argue with a word of it.

'There has come a time, Luke, a time for change.'

He was trying to look into my eyes. I avoided his glare.

'Look at me,' he said. The authority in his voice, the first time in three years that I had heard it, had a new effect on me. I could feel my cock hardening.

Slowly, bashfully, I obeyed.

I looked up.

He waited.

I tried to pull myself together, holding myself upright and proud.

'That's better, boy,' he said.

I wondered if I had heard him correctly. He didn't give me any more time to think about it.

'As I say, Luke, for three years I have had you watching me, in the gym, the pool, running. I won't say I haven't been flattered. I have been. And, I have been frustrated. Now, I think it's about time I did something about it. But you, Luke, have a choice.'

I must have looked surprised.

'Yes,' he said, 'that's right, a choice. I'm not sure if you'll like it, but then that's not important, at least to you.'

I suddenly felt very small, humiliated. I wondered where this was going.

The atmosphere had become very sexual.

I could feel my cock fully erect now. Mr Benini knew it. He could see it. He said nothing about it. He was enjoying my discomfort. The embarrassment had changed places. He waited.

'Yes,' he said, a few moments later, 'the choice is very simple, Luke.'

He waited again.

'Either you apologize," he paused, 'properly," he hesitated again, letting me appreciate his choice of word, 'or I punish you.'

He waited for me to appreciate what he had said. He looked at me again.

'Or there again, I could punish you anyway, or punish you because I didn't think the apology was sufficiently fulsome. Which is it to be?'

I said nothing. I knelt as slowly and carefully as I could. I wanted my apology to have some dignity to it.

As soon as I was kneeling, I bowed my head.

My hands stayed behind my back.

I inched myself towards Mr Benini. I could see the bulge in his tight shorts twitching. His feet were bare. When I felt myself close enough, I bent back onto my haunches and then forwards. I kissed one foot then the other. Then, I let my tongue start working. I knew not to rush. I felt that however slowly I went, it would be too fast. I tried to slow down. I was panting. This contact was something that I'd been waiting for too. I'd thought it would never come. Now it had, I'd been caught by surprise. I was fighting hard to focus.

I licked between each toe, as carefully as I could. If Mr Benini wanted an apology, he could have one, but it would be a slow, frustrating one. It took me quite some time. I put aside my plans for starting the drive back home for a while. I worked each foot, slowly, lovingly. This was something I'd wanted for three years, something I never thought I'd have. I didn't know whether I would ever have it again. I didn't want to waste a second. I wanted it to last forever.

I could feel my cock as hard as a rock. I was wearing Speedos under my jeans. I'd planned to get rid of the denim and my tee-shirt as soon as I'd cleared town and drive wearing nothing but the Speedos. It sure was a hot – and cool – way to drive. I had visions of enjoying the reactions of the truck drivers, as they looked down and saw what was there. The few times I'd done it in the past, I'd always made sure I'd wore stripes, just to make the profile that bit more obvious. Truck stops had been fun too, I remembered.

I wondered if Mr Benini was appreciating my attention. I opened my eyes a little as I worked my mouth up his legs. He was lying back now, his eyes closed. I could see up the legs of his shorts. At last, I thought, I know. He was wearing a jock. The bulge in it had grown significantly. I smiled and kept my tongue working. I brought my hands from behind my back and started working the skin where I had already licked. I ran my fingertips gently up and down his calves, up to the back of his knees.

Slowly, I approached the shorts. I made a deliberate effort to run my tongue in long sweeps from his knees. I tickled the end of my tongue in, under the fabric. I was caught by surprise when Mr Benini suddenly stood up. He pushed me backwards. I had to put my hands back quickly to stay kneeling.

'Take them off, boy,' he said, sternly, 'but don't use your hands.'

I went to it. I grasped the waist band of the shorts in my teeth and pulled it downwards. I had to move round him to get it over the mound in his jockstrap and over the curves of his muscled butt. I licked each buttock as I did. They were firm, outlined where the tan met the white area that had been covered in the sun. They were dimpled too. I tried to work my tongue a little between the cheeks. There was a taste of perspiration. It was good.

I moved in front of him again. I pulled the shorts down to his knees and then licked all the way up each thigh. I ran my tongue round behind the pouch, outlining his balls. I could see his cock, strong and erect, but imprisoned by the material of the jockstrap. It was long and thick. I wondered if I would be able to take it all into my mouth. I started licking, first the balls, wetting the fabric, teasing the skin of the sac with the end of my tongue. Then I ran the tip up and down his cock, teasing the end, making circles around the piss slit. I ran my hands up and down his thighs and gently, but firmly, kneaded the delicious hemispheres of his butt.

The fabric was getting nicely damp. I could feel Mr Benini's cock twitching. It felt so good. I kept my mouth busy as he stepped out of the shorts. I hoped I was apologizing well enough for him. I bent and ran my tongue into the crevice behind his balls, between his legs. The sweat there tasted fresh and masculine. I sucked as much as I could from the skin.

I ran my fingers into the crevice between his buttocks. I was touching his hole. It responded. I liked that. The twitch of the sphincter was a good indication that Coach Benini's hole was accustomed to attention. It was clean but damp with sweat. I wanted to get my tongue there too. I was starting to work towards grasping the waistband with my mouth when Mr Benini stopped me.

He put his hands under my shoulders and lifted me until I was standing. He said nothing. He moved me to the front of his desk. There were three white cards there. I saw them then for the first time. He nodded, indicating that I should pick one. I obeyed. I turned it over. There was a number – twelve.

Mr Benini was beside me then. I could feel the hardness still of his cock in his jockstrap. He nodded again, indicating that I should put my hands on the edge of the desk. He kicked my feet back and apart. It was only then that he went behind me and undid my jeans. I knew what was coming by then. My cock was still as hard as a rock. Mr Benini ran his hand against my erection as he undid my fly and pulled my jeans down over my butt. I felt him rub the material of the Speedos across my buttocks. I couldn't see his expression, but it was as if he hadn't expected them and liked what he saw. I thought he was going to pull them down too.

He didn't. The Speedos were still in place when I felt the paddle rubbing gently against my butt. There was a tension in the air, I could feel it. I knew I wanted to be there; no, I needed to be there. I could feel Mr Benini behind me. I could smell his perspiration in the warm air; it was fresh and masculine. I tried to prepare myself for the blow which was coming. I didn't say anything. I tried to control my breathing and push my ass back to give him an easier, clearer target.

Even so, the first impact caught me by surprise, more from its intensity than its timing. I felt the muscles in my face and neck move, but no sound came out. I wanted to shriek, but it was as if my brain had obediently switched off my vocal chords. Mr Benini was putting his strength behind the paddle. I shouted, but no sound came out. I was still thinking about how my body had reacted when the second stroke landed.

It hurt. So too did the others. Mr Benini was counting them. As soon as the second stroke had hit me, I'd realized that my cock had shrunk. It wasn't until about the eighth or ninth, when I had become more accustomed to the sensations that my erection began to return. I had learned by then, even so quickly, that there was a furious intensity when the paddle hit, but that it was sudden and short. The fury very soon became a hot glow. The transformation could occur between the impact of one stroke and the next, as Mr Benini lifted the paddle and bringing it down again. I knew I could endure the fire of those milliseconds after the contact. I could hear Mr Benini breathing more quickly by then. The aroma of his sweat was greater too.

The last stroke hit me. I stood still. I wasn't sure quite what to do. If Mr Benini wanted to be in charge, then he could give the orders, I thought. I didn't have to wait long. I could feel him rubbing my ass. I stood still, resting my hands on the desk as he reached round in front of me and felt my erection.

'It's good to know you appreciate my efforts, Luke,' he said as he ran his hand up and down my hardening cock. I could feel my balls tightening too. I held my position as he pulled on the drawstring of the Speedos and pulled them down. The thin fabric had been no protection.

Mr Benini turned me round. He pushed me back on to the desk. I didn't resist the bigger man. I laid back on his desk, my butt just on the edge. I could see him now. He'd taken off the tanktop. I was fascinated by the broad chest. I always did like men with defined pecs. Coach Benini had worked hard for that physique. He reached for his shorts and pulled a condom from the pocket. He looked amazing, standing there wearing only a jock, his cock pushing hard against the fabric of the pouch.

I could feel a draught against the heat of my butt as he moved around. I had brought my knees up on to my stomach. I knew exactly what would happen next.

'That's just part of my due, Luke,' Mr Benini said as he pushed the jockstrap down his muscled thighs. I knew. I was ready to pay the rest. I felt my mouth fall open as I saw Mr Benini's cock for the first time. I knew it would not be the last. It was big. It was thick. It was uncut. What was more amazing to me was the heavy steel ring implanted in the head. I could see it emerging from his piss-slit. Mr Benini noticed my gaze. He smiled. I wondered how it would feel.

'Get ready boy,' he said.

I didn't have to wait long. I watched as Mr Benini carefully unrolled the condom over the ring and pulled it down his cock. I looked around. I could see no grease. I'd never taken a piece of metal like that. I wondered if the condom would be strong enough. I wondered what the steel would feel like inside me.

Again, Mr Benini followed my eyes.

'That's right, Luke,' he said. 'No help, only what's already on the condom.'

I was scared then. I'd been fucked before, many times by then. I'd even been fisted a couple of times, but always with grease, lots of grease. Mr Benini smiled as he came towards me. I could feel the heat in my ass get more intense as his pelvis pressed against me. I could feel the latex-sheathed tip of his cock tickle my hole.

I looked straight into his eyes as he bent forward over me. He put his hands to each side of me. He leaned forward and brought his lips down on to mine. His tongue pushed my mouth open. For a second, I closed my eyes. As I did, he pushed hard. By the time my eyes had shot open again, he had shoved the entirety of his erection into me. I felt the lust in my eyes hit his retinas. I let go of the desk. I threw my arms round him. I squeezed him, hard. I started sucking on his tongue as if it was a cock. I started working the muscles of my ass, tensing and relaxing, tensing and relaxing.

I think my passion surprised him. It was a moment before he picked up on my rhythm and started pumping my ass. He pulled back until only the head of his cock, that big round, steel-carrying, mushroom head, was inside me. Then he slammed home again. He did that several times. It was as if he was making sure that I knew he was there, that he was taking my ass, claiming it as his own.

I could feel my erection again, he was rubbing against it as he fucked me and I sucked his tongue. I could feel the bristles of Mr Benini's hair against the welts of my butt as he thrust into me. I was getting scared. I wondered how long I could endure what was happening. I could feel each jolt against my prostate. I could feel pre-cum starting to ooze from my own cock, lubricating the rubbing of Mr Benini's body. I tried to focus, to concentrate on that. I could feel more stubble rubbing against me. I wondered how sore my cock would be.

I was trying to suck Mr Benini's tongue from out of his mouth and, at the same time, grit my teeth as the intensity and frequency of his thrusts grew. Then, with as much of a roar as my attention to his tongue would allow, Mr Benini pulled back. There was one last, greatest, intense thrust. This time the head of his cock did not pull back from my prostate. It stayed there, compressing it, forcing pre- cum through me.

There was a tension in all Mr Benini's muscles. He was holding me tighter. His chest was pressed down more heavily on me. My cock was trapped. I hadn't realized that it had started its own pumping by then. I let go of Mr Benini's tongue and tried to throw my head back. He wouldn't let me. He clamped his mouth down on mine even harder. He was filling me with his spit.

We held that moment. I could feel Mr Benini's cock inside me. I gently used my muscles to squeeze it gently inside me. It felt so glorious. After the power of the fuck, I was surprised by the care and sensitivity when he pulled out of me. I suddenly felt very empty. I had forgotten about the welts on my butt, I could only feel the air against my hole.

It wasn't empty for long. I was still panting, lying on the desk when I felt something even harder than Mr Benini's cock against my hold. I raised my head and tried to see. Mr Benini bent forward and putting his mouth over mine, pushed my head back.

'Stay there, Luke,' he said.

It was an order. I could feel my ass being opened again,

then suddenly the muscle relaxed a little. It took me a moment before I realized he'd filled me with a plug. My eyes opened. I started to protest. Again Mr Benini stopped me. He held his hand against my mouth.

He pulled me forward until I was standing. I hadn't noticed until then, but he'd pulled on my Speedos. They looked good on him. Silently, he handed me his jockstrap. I could feel the plug embedded deep in my ass as I bent forward to put it on. Despite only just having come, my cock was hard at attention again already. Mr Benini rubbed my stomach with a towel.

I stood wearing only the jockstrap and the plug while Mr Benini pulled some chinos on over the Speedos. I could already see his cock hardening again. I wondered if I'd ever see them again. I watched, disappointedly, as he pulled on a shirt, covering the magnificent definition of his chest and back.

He handed me an envelope.

He spoke at last.

'It's two o'clock now, Luke. You have a simple choice. Either be back here at five, having read and signed what is in that envelope, or I never want to see you again. Lock the door behind you when you leave.'

With that, he was gone.

I was standing there, alone in his office, apart from his own jockstrap and with an envelope in my hand and a plug in my ass.

* * *

It took me a few moments to appreciate what had happened. I'd loved it. I was still hard. I pulled off the jockstrap and held it close to my nose. I sniffed it. I licked it. I wanted to savor the aroma and the taste of Mr Benini.

I was so into the jockstrap that for a moment I forgot the envelope, even though it was on the desk beside me. I saw it and wondered what was inside. Reluctantly, I put down the jockstrap. I opened the envelope carefully and gently. There was something about it which made me respect it. Perhaps it was just because it came from Mr Benini.

There wasn't a lot of writing on the first sheet. It was short and very much to the point.

'I've noticed your behavior," Mr Benini had written. 'I think you have great slave potential, young man. If you want a permanent position, as my assistant, but with very strict conditions, you have until 5pm today to read and sign the enclosed contract.

'If you wish to accept this offer, you will be here at five. After that you may return to your home for five days. You will return here at the end of the week. You will have a room of your own, in my quarters. This arrangement will be for a minimum of one year, to be reviewed and renewed after that.'

I didn't need to read the contract. I knew I would be accepting it. I looked at the clock on the wall. It was 2.07. I had less than three hours. I tried to calm down and plan what I was going to do.

And that, Andrew, is how it all started. That afternoon, I became Mr Benini's assistant and slave. I met Professor Donaldson for the first time at the start of the next semester; he had come to the university for that year. He and Mr Benini were old friends. Mr Benini sent me to the Professor at Christmastime when he went home to his own family. It was a further joy. When Professor Donaldson decided to move, the following summer, I left with him. My contract with Mr Benini was not renewed and I moved here.

That was just under two years ago now.

Luke and Brandon

'I smiled then', said Andrew. He reached for my hand. The scene had returned to Andrew and Ross. I had to remember who I was for a moment.

The story was coming full circle. Each boy's education and experience was being passed on. Each was learning from the others, from what they'd endured and what they'd thought, how their minds had worked as much as their bodies.

Sitting there, in the coffee shop as Andrew relayed Luke's story, was a revelation. Andrew was as naive as Luke had been in his teens. He knew that later, probably in bed, he would be trying again to relate his life to Luke's.

So much more made sense. There were still questions Andrew wanted to ask. The time, Andrew decided would come in due course. Luke had provided so much to think about, but he hadn't finished.

Andrew was trying to understand what he had told me about Luke, what that young man had said, his thoughts and his feelings, about his time with Rob, his Dad, and Mr Benini. Luke had had so much experience so quickly. Andrew knew that these men meant a lot to Luke, and also indirectly to him because of their example, but he didn't know how or why. As they talked, Andrew could feel himself become increasingly envious.

'I was confused when you were telling me all that,' Andrew told me. 'I was thinking about Mary, about married life, about my own children, about my sexuality. Did respectable middle-aged men have such feelings, I wondered. Did they behave like that?

'I supposed they did,' he went on, almost talking to himself. 'They must do. It was probably just that I'd never seen them before. If I'd met them, I hadn't seen that side of them. Perhaps simply because I hadn't known what to look for, the signs and the clues, I'd never noticed and those people, their needs and their behaviors had been there all the time.

'I'd seen men who were camp and effeminate. If that was what being gay was all about then I definitely knew that wasn't me. Even Mary knew that. I knew from the homes of some of our friends that there were men who were sleeping in bedrooms with flowered wall coverings, on lace-trimmed sheets; that wasn't for me either. The asexual me wasn't like that. It was more gender neutral, if you will. Mary appreciated that. I don't think she was into the flowery either. The clothes she chose for herself were patterned, but never what some people would describe as overtly, sexually, "feminine".

'Luke had started me thinking, reviewing so much of my life. He'd started a process. Probably without realizing what he was doing he had shown me that there was a different perspective from the one I'd been using, unchallenged, and passively, for so many years. He'd shone a new light on life for me. It was stronger, may be even a different color. It was certainly coming from a different direction.

'I started wondering about the significance of some of my likes and dislikes. I'd loved Mary, but I suddenly realized that I'd never really seen her as a sexual being. She was certainly never a sex "object". I wondered if my dislike of the frilly and the lacy came from an underlying dislike of the "feminine". I couldn't see Mary as "butch". I could see a woman, matronly, maternal, caring and competent. She didn't look masculine. Yes, she could keep control, she did know what she was doing; she could manage and organize. I felt uneasy, thinking about what Luke had said, wondering whether I'd been dishonest with her for so many years. No, I thought, she was perceptive too. If there had been something there, she would have noticed. She would have found the right time and said something, or asked me about it. She did that. Usually, I didn't notice immediately, but she'd say something, and then, a few hours later, perhaps the next day, I'd appreciate what she'd said and how it had taken me down a path of reasoning that I hadn't previously thought about. It was if she knew that there was an option missing from my deliberations and that she had to put up the first signpost so I could set off along the trek of intellectual exploration that I had to travel to find the answers I needed.

'She was so perceptive in that way that if there had been anything that she'd found even remotely uncomfortable about me, about my thinking and behavior, she'd have done just that. She'd have asked that throw-away question, just when one of us was leaving a room, like a medic who tells you to pinch yourself just as the needle is going in; you're distracted and miss the significance of the moment. "I found how I thought about Donaldson was changing too. I no longer saw him as a peer, an equal, but appreciated the dominance and control in his demeanor. I wasn't sure he was the right person to talk to either. I didn't know how much empathy he would have with my emotions, my predicament.

'It was Luke who provided me with that,' said Andrew. The flashback had started again.

He'd found me, after dinner that night, sitting beside the pool, said Andrew. Donaldson had left us and gone inside to work, to make some calls, I can't remember what exactly. Luke had been gone for some time too, clearing up. I'd been sitting, trying to work through my thoughts, there were so many of them and they seemed to be going off in so many directions at once that I was getting edgy, I was pleased, relieved, when he came back. He brought a bottle and filled my glass.

'So,' he'd said, 'a penny for them?'

He'd knelt on the edge of the pool beside me. He was wearing only his collar and Speedos again. He looked so beautiful. I envied him his peace too. He had discovered an important part of himself. He knew where he was going, what he was doing, what he needed.

I looked at him.

'There are so many,' I said, answering his first question, 'that I'd probably drain your savings.'

It was his turn to smile. He reached for my hand. It was the supportive and affectionate gesture I needed. He looked at me, deep into my eyes. It was as if he was trying to read my mind. He looked at me questioningly, as if requesting permission to speak.

'Yes?' I said, hoping he would shed some more light on what was happening inside my brain.

'Are you sure?' he said. 'Are you ready?'

I took a deep breath.

'I don't think I really have a choice with this one, Luke,' I said. 'If I don't hear what you have to say, I could be trying to put a lid on something which is better let out. You've given me so much to think about, and so much has changed in my life recently, that I don't think I really have any option but to go with the flow.'

I was tense. I wasn't sure if I really did want to hear more from Luke, but there was a voice inside me telling me to listen, that I hadn't had such an opportunity to hear anything so important for many years and that I'd be a fool to deny myself the possibility of a great discovery now.

'Okay,' he said. 'I think you already know the answer though.'

I looked at him. Perhaps I did.

'You'll never really know until you try it.'

I closed my eyes, took a deep breath and nodded.

'You mustn't, you shouldn't, say no until you have experienced something, should you?'

He was squeezing my hand more firmly now.

Luke was good. He didn't rush me. He let me think. As with so much in life, it wasn't taking the decision that was difficult. The decision took itself. The choice had been made. The route had been planned. It was accepting and appreciating the implications that were harder.

'It'll be hard,' Luke said, 'but then I think you already know that.'

I nodded.

'Physically and psychologically,' he added, 'but then I think you have the strength to cope.'

He paused.

'Otherwise,' he said slowly, looking into my eyes, 'you wouldn't still be here and we certainly wouldn't be having this conversation.'

'So,' I said, 'what do you recommend?'

It was Luke's turn to smile.

'You really want to know?'

I nodded.

'I do,' I said. 'Tell me.'

Luke grinned.

'There's only one word for it,' he said.

He was teasing me then. I squeezed his hand and smiled.

'I think we both know it,' I said, looking at him for confirmation.

'Experience,' we said together.

'You've got it,'' Luke said, 'I'm pleased you realized that for yourself. You know I'll hold your hand, don't you?'

I squeezed his wrist.

'Yes,' I said, slowly, 'I do. But I also don't know how to get that experience, what to do.'

'Well, you could start here,' Luke said.

I shook my head.

'Tempting as that offer is,' I said, 'it wouldn't work. It would be wrong. I know I'm seeing Donaldson differently, but, well, certainly not yet, I still see him more as a colleague than as a Master, but my perspective has started to change.'

Luke could see how uneasy I was.

'Yes, he is attractive. I like his confidence too, but ....' My voice trailed off.

'You don't need to say any more, Andrew,' Luke said.

It was the first time he had used my name on its own. It was if he was saying welcome to the world of the slave. I was touched, honored by him.

'There are some people with whom you know, instinctively, that it would be wrong. You've been too close, or you know them from a different context, one where changing the roles so significantly could cause problems. That's an important lesson to learn, he said. 'It has to be consensual

'There are some people who think you have to say yes, deliberately, consciously, expressly, every time a master wants you to do something,' he went on. 'Others say it's perfectly possible to consent for significant periods of time, a month, a year, perhaps even more. I prefer that. My consent to the Professor was for a year at first. Now it's for three years.'

I nodded. It made sense to me too.

'So,' I said, fishing again for information, 'how do I find such experience?'

Luke smiled.

I could see the gleam in his eye, even as the darkness fell.

'It's called either networking or a small world,' he said. 'It's who you know.'

I looked puzzled.

'But I don't know anyone,' I said.

Luke grinned.

'Oh yes you do,' he said. 'You do already. You know the Professor,' he paused, 'and you know me.'

'I couldn't ask Donaldson,' I said. 'Even that wouldn't seem right.'

I was looking into the distance then. Luke reached for my hand and my attention.

'You could ask me,' he said. I smiled. 'But you need to ask, Andrew. You have to say it, out loud, deliberately. I'm not going to accept what you've already said as a request.'

I looked at him.

He was already challenging me. His statement made me appreciate why I couldn't ask Donaldson. My prejudices were getting in the way. He wouldn't, he shouldn't, I reckoned, think any less of me, value me any less as a colleague and friend if I was honest about my emotions and my growing needs. Were those needs growing, I wondered, or had they always been there and it was only my awareness of them which was increasing? Luke was being patient.

'Whenever you're ready,' he said. 'It's up to you. You know the deal, I think. I won't say no and once you ask the process is under way.'

I nodded.

It took me a few moments more to compose myself. I turned and got out of the chair. I knelt on the poolside in front of Luke. I reached for both his hands. I looked him directly in the eyes.

'Luke,' I said, 'will you please help me find my first experience ...' I had to pause, trying to get the words out of my mouth, '... as a slave.'

It was out. I was almost panting. There were tears in the side of my eyes. I was surprised when Luke leaned forward and kissed me deliberately and carefully, but without lingering, on the lips.

'Of course,' he said. 'Thank you for asking. It will be a privilege.'

He smiled.

'I think, Andrew,' he said, 'you will be a natural.'

I was surprised. He noticed my confusion.

'Look at what you have just done,' he said. 'This little ritual, turning, facing, holding me, kneeling, while you asked. That's an action of a good slave, an action that a good master should like and appreciate.'

He quickly squeezed my hand and was just about to let go when Donaldson appeared.

I can remember his look to this day. He wasn't surprised. That was what amazed me. Luke immediately and obediently froze. I didn't know what to do with myself. I couldn't go anywhere, couldn't stand as Luke was still holding my hands, tightly. I could see him smiling. It was as if we were naughty children, having been caught with our hands illicitly in the biscuit barrel or raiding an apple orchard.

Donaldson walked over to us. He bent and kissed my forehead and ran his hand through the stubble on my head. He grinned. He took my hands from Luke's and helped me stand up.

'My only doubt was how long this would take,' he said, looking me directly in the eye. I couldn't help myself any longer. I burst into tears. I put my arms round his chest and wept. I suddenly felt free.

Donaldson let me cry for a few moments and then guided me to sit beside him on a bench.

'Andrew,' he said at last, putting his hand under my chin and looking into my eyes.

'Yes?' I said, wondering what was coming, whether he was going to take me there and then, and make me his slave.

'No,' Donaldson said, reading my mind. 'I'm not the right person, at least not yet.'

We both smiled.

'Maybe one day,' he went on. 'You have a good body, it can be better though, and one day perhaps, I'd like to use it, but that day is still some way away.'

I squeezed his hand. It was an action I liked, I needed, especially when I was emotionally stressed. I'd been doing a lot of it, I realized.

'Luke is going to help,' I said, then suddenly adding, 'if that's okay with you?'

The etiquette and protocol would take some remembering, if not always some learning, I thought.

'Yes, that's ideal,' Donaldson said. 'I'm not sure what I can contribute, or what it would be appropriate for me to contribute, but do please feel free to ask, at least for the time being.'

It was another indication that our relationship had started changing. I reached for my glass. I wondered if I should have asked permission.

'I'm nervous,' I said, 'scared.'

Donaldson looked at me, seeking clarification.

'Scared?' he asked, 'of what?'

I waited for a moment before answering.

'I'm not sure,' I said, 'of myself, I think, of what's inside, of what's being let out, and, well, also of us. I'm not sure I know how to behave towards you any more.'

Donaldson smiled again.

'Let's let that develop as it will, Andrew,' he said. 'You're still a guest in my home, that's not changed. Do as you wish to do. If you want any changes, then say so, either to me or to Luke.'

And that is how it started. I found it difficult to talk to Donaldson. There was something about our intimacy that made it more appropriate, easier, for me to talk to Luke. He was the one who took charge of my education.

I wasn't sure what more I could say to Donaldson that night. He'd caught me, discovered me at my most exposed, my most vulnerable. I appreciate the fact that he hadn't abused that in any way. We sat for a while, and talked. Luke occasionally filled our glasses. The conversation I remember was bland. I was uneasy. I escaped to bed as soon as I could.

When I got to my room, I found a book on the nightstand. Luke must have put it there for me. It was called Entertainment for a Master. I took off the skimpy shorts that I'd been wearing and climbed under the sheet. It was a warm night.

Much to consider

It was nearly dawn when I finished reading. The book hadn't taken that long; it was that several times during the night I had had to stop and think. If I'd been told even two or three days earlier that I would have spent the night reading a book like that, I'd have laughed it off; I might even have been offended. I hoped I wasn't trying to move too quickly, so much had happened to me since I'd arrived at Donaldson's home. I wondered if I should find some paper and write down my thoughts and reactions to the book. I decided against that.

I'd closed the bedroom door soon after I'd started reading. I didn't want to disturb Donaldson, or Luke, and I didn't really want to be disturbed by either of them as I read. There were aspects of the text I found disconcerting. I could appreciate the eroticism of the hard male bodies, the desire to provide sexual service for another person. I couldn't understand the pain. There had been so many images, so many concepts, that my brain was still spinning.

I moved as soon as I heard a noise indicating that the house was coming to life for the new day. I knew when I opened the door that it was Luke. I could see a light in his room. I left my door open and went back to my bed. A moment later he was there, in the doorway.

'Thank you,' I said, 'for letting me read the John Preston.'

I held it out for him.

'You've finished it?' he said. 'Already?'

I nodded.

He came into the room then and took the book. He put it down.

'And?' he asked.

I smiled.

'And,' I said, 'it has given me a lot to think about, an awful lot.'

'Such as?' he said.

'I'm not sure,' I replied. 'I can appreciate a lot of the emotions. It took me a while to appreciate that while the guy appears at first to be writing from the perspective of the top, the master, he really has an insight into the psychology of the bottoms, the slaves. It reads more like the-master-I-never-had-but-would- really-have-liked,' I said. 'I could appreciate aspects of each of the men he described.'

Luke came and sat on the bed then, and smiled.

'Good,' he said. 'There are others in the series, you should read those too, and some other books, not novels. I'll prepare a list, get them ready for you.'

I reached for his hand and held it for a moment.

'Luke,' I said, 'I know I'm keen, but please don't rush me. I have almost too much to think about already.'

He looked at me apologetically.

'I'm sorry,' he said, 'my enthusiasm sometimes gets the better of me.'

I grinned.

'I understand,' I said. 'It's not that I haven't figured out what's going on or that I'm not grateful, it's, well, it's just that, you know, I have so much to think about. It's only a couple of days since I met you for the first time, and here I am, having shared some of my most intimate feelings with you, feelings that until a day or so ago, I didn't even knew I had.'

'It's like that,' he said.

I looked puzzled.

'Our world,' he explained, 'especially for slaves, we find ourselves in situations which are almost the complete opposite of conventional life. We find ourselves sharing the most intimate, extreme, esoteric sexual experiences with guys, men, we have never met, perhaps never seen before. We have to get along with them, we may never be introduced. We may never know their names. We may never have a chance to get to know them, what they have achieved professionally, intellectually. Others, well, they meet each other, where, through work, or in a bar, perhaps, through the country club? They find out about each other's professional and cultural interests and skills. They are like dogs, very slowly sniffing round each other trying to decide whether they can use each other or how much they will trust each other. They have facades that are so thick. They may never let anyone else know what they are really thinking, even their wives.'

I nodded. I remembered one of the characters in the book; he was like that.

'Eventually, perhaps over ten, maybe even twenty years or more, they will slowly get to know someone. They may never have a friend, a real friend, someone who will value them for who they are, not what they are, who will love them, find time for them, and never think any less of them, regardless of what happens to them in their lives. They may have acquaintances, sure, but friends? No, I doubt it.

I knew what Luke was describing. He may have been thirty years my junior, in age terms, but there was a wisdom and knowledge on his shoulders which impressed me. I don't think it shocked me. I wondered for a moment what my life would have brought if I'd discovered that aspect of myself when I'd been so young. I banished the idea. There was no way I could ever know. Even thinking about the idea would do me no good. If this was a part of me, a real part of me, I had to start to live with it now, to explore it, to try and understand it perhaps, to express it, I hoped, and to grow with it.

'You and I, Andrew,' said Luke, 'we're already far far closer than many of the people who we'll see today, out and about. You are closer to Donaldson than you are to many others, even though you might not realize it,' he said.

I nodded. I was already starting to appreciate what he meant.

'So,' I asked, 'how do I go forward? What do I do? What should I know? There seems so much to discover.'

Luke smiled.

'What there is is probably inside you already, it's just that you haven't realized it's there before now,' he said. 'Doing what feels right is important, just as you knelt when you asked me for help last night.'

I was suddenly embarrassed by being reminded. Had I really asked that question? Did I really want it to happen?

Luke read my mind.

'If you don't give it a go,' he said, 'you'll never know what it was like, or could have been like, and you'll spend the rest of your life wondering, regretting that you didn't take the opportunity you had to find out.

'I made a call last night,' he said, 'after you'd come to bed. You don't have to go home, back to the West Coast, for a while, do you?'

I shook my head.

'I can be away as long as I want,' I said, feeling that at one and the same time I had a great new freedom which I was immediately sacrificing.

Luke smiled.

'Good,' he said, 'I've arranged for you to go and spend a few days with an old friend of mine the weekend after next. That gives us ten days to get you ready.'

Luke and Andrew

I was still taking in the news when I realized that Luke had gone. I could feel my cock and balls shrinking, yet there was a tumescence in my cock at the same time. I wondered what I had let myself in for.

Andrew was continuing his story. There was so much to it, but every detail was relevant. To understand him, and learn from him, he had to reveal everything. His Master, Lord Cunningham, had given Andrew a couple of hours to himself that afternoon. His Lordship was sitting back under the trees, enjoying a post-prandial cigar, the conversation of others and the tongue of a near-naked law student from Harvard on his boots.

My mind was racing when Luke came back, continued Andrew. He threw some Speedos and a cock ring down on the bed and went and turned the shower on.

'Are you ready?' he asked, as he came back towards me.

'Do you want an honest answer to that?' I said, as he stood beside me.

'Give me both the honest and dishonest ones,' he responded, 'but come with me.'

I got out of bed. My cock was hardening even though it wasn't erect.

'The really honest single answer is that I don't know,' I said. 'I'm excited, but scared that it could be real, and even more scared that I could be enjoying it.'

Luke said nothing as he stepped into the shower after me. He didn't take off the Speedos, I noticed. I hadn't seen that he had a razor in his hand until he turned me round towards him. Carefully, under the warm running water, he started work. I didn't stop him. Instinctively, I put my hands behind my back and tried to keep as still as I could. He worked his way from my face all the way down my body. My cock was hard by the time he reached my groin. The way he held my cock out to one side was almost clinical as he removed the hair. It was only when he was finished, had rubbed my skin carefully to make sure that it was smooth that he showed any emotion. He bent down and quickly kissed the head of my cock. Then, almost before he'd touched it, he was standing again, right in front of me.

He looked me directly in the eyes. My cock was really hard now, my balls drawn up in their sac. I was excited. Luke smiled at me.

'You are not to touch that cock, Andrew,' he said.

My jaw dropped.

He grinned, almost sadistically.

'You may only shake it after you've pissed, that's what the Master you'll be seeing next week has said.'

I was incredulous. I wondered what other instructions had been issued.

'You are to wear a cock ring every day. I am to shave you every second day. You will wear the same type of Speedos or shorts as me. You are not to remove them if you only want to piss. You are to sit and piss through them.'

Luke noticed my astonishment.

'Don't worry,' he said, 'the weather's warm; they'll have dried out before you notice it. You're to sleep in the Speedos too. I have a workout schedule for you. From the weekend, you are to sleep in my room, on the floor with me.'

I wasn't sure what to say. My cock was still hard as Luke leaned forward and kissed me.

'See,' he said, tapping my erection, 'something is saying you're doing the right thing.'

He led me out of the shower and put my hands behind my back. He let me dry just standing there as he made the bed. He was right, drying didn't take long. I stayed still as he fought to pull a rubber ring around my cock and balls. He bent down so I could step into the black bikini Speedos. He didn't make any attempt to hide my hard cock. He just left it sticking out of the top. He bent and kissed it, teasing me once more.

'It'll find its own way home,' he said.

I learned a lot from Luke during the ten days that followed. I read a lot too. Donaldson had to work most days, so that Luke and I were in the house alone together. He made sure that I worked out. I hadn't exercised deliberately, in a planned way, for many years. I wasn't in bad shape, but

Luke drew up a schedule – crunches, running, swimming and using weights for my chest and back. He also watched what I ate. He measured me and weighed me every day. I felt embarrassed the first time. I was standing beside the pool, still damp from swimming when he did it. Donaldson had come in then too. He seemed to know in advance when something would be happening to me. He'd kissed me and patted me on the arm. Luke had started a diary too. He wrote down everything in it. I was to take it with me when I went away too, he said.

He hadn't told me then where I'd be going, or who I'd be going to see. Somehow that didn't matter. I knew that Luke wouldn't have contacted someone whom he didn't trust and respect. I didn't like to ask. There had been no mention of cost, so I didn't think it was too far away.

The weekend was fun. Donaldson had two parties.

On the Saturday, there were drinks and a barbecue for some of his colleagues from the university.

Luke rose to the occasion.

Some of the guests thought he was a live-in butler, others a hired caterer. He'd selected what he had told me were 'dance belts' for us to wear that day, the thongs that male ballet dancers wear under their tights. I'd expected them to be a little like a jockstrap, but soon remembered that they were far more constraining, holding one's cock and balls right up out of the way and allowing no movement whatsoever. It felt strange but wonderful under my chinos. Luke was deliciously wicked; he'd brush against my crotch or butt whenever he could; I felt he made a determined effort to pass me every time he brought a new tray of glasses or canapés into the room. He looked good himself. The vest he had chosen seemed to emphasize the size of his shoulders and upper arms, accentuate the V shape of his back and the narrowness of his waist. He'd chosen black trousers that looked as if they had been sprayed on, yet somehow they didn't look obscene.

The effect was quite beautiful – and he knew it. Donaldson knew it too. Just as Luke was making every opportunity to tease me, Donaldson would tap the bulge at the front of Luke's trousers on every occasion he could. I could see him gritting his teeth behind the courteousness of his smile whenever a tap or a punch hit home.

* * *

Sunday's event was more select. Luke wore only a dance belt, white this time. He'd put one out for me too. There were no trousers, vest or shirt. The garment fitted over his cock and balls like an extra skin

I watched that morning as he'd knelt beside Donaldson at the breakfast table. An elegant steel collar had been locked in place around his neck. In the early afternoon, shortly before the first guests were due to arrive, Luke again knelt. This time, steel bracelets, polished like mirrors were fixed around each wrist. A chain was passed behind his back linking the two bands. It was long enough to allow him to carry a tray, but not to let him touch his cock or bring his hands together. Steel bands were also locked around each bicep, his thighs and between his ankles. He did look impressive.

Donaldson appeared as I'd never seen him before. He wore some beautifully tailored leather pants and a steel harness over his shoulders and just below his rib cage. It gave him an almost mythical appearance. I could imagine him as a Norse god; all that seemed to be missing was a helmet with horns.

'You look amazing,' I said quietly to him, as we waited for the guests to arrive.

'Thank you,' Donaldson replied, 'you look good yourself, Andrew. How are you feeling?'

It was the first time he had asked me for three days.

'I'm becoming more comfortable,' I said. It was true. Even though I was only wearing the tight white pouch and a cockring, I was feeling good. Luke had shaved me again that morning and my skin felt fresh against the warm afternoon sunshine. I didn't dare think of how I would have reacted a week earlier if I'd been told what I would have been doing, nor did I add that my ordered restraint was making me extremely horny.

'You'll meet some interesting people this afternoon,' Donaldson explained. 'It may be a good idea if you watched them arrive.'

I took the hint.

I had thought of going to my room, but I wouldn't know who any of the callers were. I found myself a position near the front door. I could just see out of a small window. Luke was in front of me. He could tell me who was who.

I was wondering why Donaldson had made the suggestion, but when the first car drew up, I knew why. I watched as a young man, not unlike Luke, jumped out of the driver's door and ran round to open the back door on the other side. Luke was watching over my shoulder. He was in butler mode, ready to open the front door, to welcome Donaldson's guests and take them through to the deck.

'That's Dean Goldstein, I recognize the car.' said Luke. 'His boy's called Hoody, short for Yehudi.'

The young man was wearing only the briefest of square-cut swimming shorts. There was a chain around his neck and boots on his feet. A taller, older man got out and walked towards the front door. That, I thought must be the Dean. Hoody ran ahead of him. I heard the bell ring, then I watched as he ran back towards the car and parked it neatly. As soon as he was through parking, Hoody walked round to the side gate.

The ritual was the same when the second car arrived. This time, however, it was the driver who was older. He was tall, quite thin, and was wearing an elegant gray double-breasted suit and chauffeur's cap. He looked exceedingly elegant. Whereas the first young man's head had been shaved, I could see a line of neatly trimmed gray hair. I watched as he too opened a passenger door.

Luke pushed me aside so he could see who was arriving.

'Dr Eldon and Brandon,' he said, before moving to be ready to open the door.

This time I saw a younger man got out of the back. That must be Dr Eldon, I thought, even though I couldn't see him too well. The older man, Brandon, held out a leather cap which Dr Eldon put on as soon as he was standing up. Dr Eldon looked as if he was in his late thirties or early forties, I guessed. His dark hair was cropped against his skull; a tight moustache and goatee beard emphasized the strength of his jaw. He looked good too, wearing tight black leather jeans and bar vest. There was a thick pelt of dark hair running down his chest and across his stomach. Even so, I could make out the definition of the pectoral and abdominal muscles. Wow, I thought, that's a hot man.

After the door bell rang and Luke took Dr Eldon through to Donaldson on the deck, I watched as the chauffeur parked the car. I had expected him to walk towards the side gate too. I was surprised when he didn't. Instead, this man, Brandon, opened the trunk, took off the cap and then the suit coat. I watched attentively and open- mouthed as he removed the polished black shoes and his socks. The black tie followed. I first noticed the collar when he undid the top button of his shirt. As far as I could see, it was steel, like Luke's. It looked good on him. I tried to work out Brandon's height as he took of the shirt. He was well over six feet tall, I guessed. I watched carefully.

I had thought at first that he was just thin, but then as I looked more carefully, I could see that he was wiry, his muscles may not have been developed, but they were highly defined. There wasn't, as far as I could make out from the distance, an ounce of body fat on him. I tried to estimate his age. He was my age, perhaps even slightly older, I thought as I watched him start to undo the pants. It had become clear to me that he had been instructed to leave the respectability of the chauffeur in the car before being allowed to come into Donaldson's house. I waited, watching the undone top button of the pants.

That was when I had the real surprise. I'm not sure what I was expecting, probably Speedos, a thong or a jockstrap, something which emphasized the cock and balls of a slave. These Masters know, Luke had told me, that something that was 'almost not there' had more effect than nakedness. Such garments remind you of your body, Luke had said, and the need to keep it beautiful, fit and ready for your Master, and of the genitals that were no longer your own to touch. I wasn't expecting steel. I watched, my mouth agape, as the man pulled down the gray suit pants. I could see the band of steel around his waist. There seemed to be a band, like a thong, running down between his buttocks. As he turned, I could see the shiny plate running from between his legs to his waist. I felt my cock react inside my own tight belt.

I was about to leave and creep through the kitchen to meet this man and find out more when the third car arrived. Luke was back by then too. This time two young men got out of the front seats. One was wearing a chain collar and tight leather shorts, nothing more. The other, who had been driving, was wearing jeans and a tight Henley-style tee-shirt. The man wearing the collar opened the rear door. Out got a thick set man. I recognized him from a photograph in Luke's room. It was Mr. Benini; Coach Benini, the man who had had such an important influence on Luke. I watched as Mr. Benini and the young man in jeans walked together towards the front door. The other young man had been waved away towards the side gate. I could see him greet the man in steel. They kissed and walked together towards the side of the house.

'As least I know one person,' I said to Luke as Mr Benini approached. 'Who are the others?'

'Joe is Coach's boy, not his slave. That's why he's allowed to come in this way,' explained Luke. 'Rick has gone round the back, with Brandon and Hoody. We can go through too now,' he added, after he had closed the door.

As he followed Mr Benini, I could see Donaldson with the others.

Donaldson beckoned me across and introduced me.

Luke was standing at one side, now, head bowed, hands behind his back.

I shook hands with Mr Benini.

'Joe,' he said, introducing me in turn to the young man in jeans.

"This,' said Donaldson, 'is Eldon, or rather Doctor Eldon now,' he joked, emphasizing the man's professional title. 'He's got his doctorate at last and is joining the faculty this coming semester. I'm sure he will make a great colleague.'

He certainly had an interesting chauffeur, I thought. I wondered what else he would be teaching. I could see the Dean more clearly now. I recognized him. I'd seen him often enough on the television nightly news, an eminent legal scholar frequently called on by the networks as a consultant for cases involving politicians or notorious businessmen.

'We've met, Sir,' I said courteously as Donaldson introduced us, 'once before, at a reception in Washington a few years ago. We both had wives with us on that occasion.' Dean Goldstein laughed politely.

'Andrew is a former colleague too,' said Donaldson, 'he's visiting and learning. I'm sure he'll appreciate the chance to talk with you more later,' he added to each of them before moving me on.

I was about to start talking more when Luke pulled me to one side.

'It's time for us to withdraw,' he said, 'like the ladies after dinner in a Jane Austen novel.'

'So aptly put, Luke,' I said quietly, struggling hard not to laugh too loudly as we moved away, leaving the Masters to themselves. His remark had brought a fresh perspective to the rites and rituals of Regency England that I'd not thought of before.

* * *

And so, we left the Masters, the tops, Donaldson, Mr Benini, Dr Eldon and Dean Goldstein, at their behest, to their own devices. Joe, as neither slave nor Master, was already in the pool.

Luke guided me out on to the deck. I shouldn't, I suppose, have been surprised, but the group of mature, otherwise respectable men kneeling on a rug there seemed somehow incongruous. They shouldn't have done, I knew, but they did. I smiled; I still had a lot to learn.

It was Luke's turn to make the introductions.

'This,' Luke said, as he led the group of us into the gym, 'is Andrew. He's an old friend of the Professor.

'I'm Hoody,' said the young man in swimming shorts.

'Rick,' said the man who had come with Mr Benini.

'And I'm Brandon,' said the man in steel.

I'd politely shaken hands with each of them, but I couldn't take my eyes off Brandon. I felt that I knew his face, but that I couldn't place him.

It was Brandon who broke the ice, ending the embarrassing silence which had fallen. He put his arm around my shoulders and hugged me.

'Welcome,' he said. 'It's years since we met last.' I was trying hard to place him. The nakedness and the steel didn't help.

'You don't remember, do you?' he asked, seeing my confusion.

'I feel I know your face,' I said, feeling ashamed of my near nakedness. Luke had been right about the intimacy; it felt distinctly unusual to come face to face with a man who had, I thought, obviously been a colleague in such circumstances.

'Don't worry,' Brandon said, steering me away from the other, younger men, 'you are Andrew Torrington, aren't you?'

I nodded.

'Yes,' I said, 'that's me.' I was still puzzled.

'Brandon Molloy,' he said. It was enough.

'Of course,' I said, 'you were on the faculty in Seattle. I should have recognized you. I am sorry.'

'You weren't to know, Andrew,' he said. 'You were too innocent.'

'I was?'

'"You were,' he replied. 'I always had suspicions. That's why I wrote to Donaldson and told him about Mary.

'It was you?' I interrupted. I'd been curious to know who had told Donaldson since that first contact.

'Yes,' Brandon confessed. He reached for my arm and held it affectionately. 'I think my suspicions were right after all,' he added, 'seeing that you're still here, and here with us now.

'I still feel bad about not recognizing you,' I said.

Brandon ... and Dr Eldon

'Don't be,' he said. 'You never had any reason to know about me when we were both out in Washington. You're seeing me in a new context, a new light. This isn't the Pacific North West. Apart from which, it's more than five years since I retired, Andrew. I've been living here on the East Coast for three.'

I looked at him, questioning him.

'Eldon was a student of mine in Washington,' he explained. 'We'd see each other out on the scene. We'd speak of course, we had dinner a few times, but, well, Andrew, you know the score, we maintained the proprieties. Sure, I found him attractive. I didn't think he'd really noticed me though, other than as one of his tutors and a social friend. We became friends. We'd talk. I introduced him to some friends, provided him with some introductions in San Francisco, as one does. We kept in touch, you know, by e-mail and on the phone, when he came here to grad school. I knew Donaldson, of course, so I made the contact for him.

I couldn't help but look down at the belt.

Brandon smiled.

'You like it?' It was a birthday gift. I'm locked in.'

My astonishment must have shown.

'Don't be worried. I can wash in it, shit in it, do just about everything in it, except get erect. I like it. It feels right,' he said.

'But,' I was searching for words ....

'Eldon, Doctor Eldon I suppose I should call him, has the keys now. See, there is this post,' he pointed to a piece of metal on the waistband, 'there's usually a piece of plastic through there, with the key on it. If there was an emergency, I could get out of quickly enough, otherwise, well, I hate to think what Eldon might do if he found I'd been tampering with it.'

I was scared, but the grin reaching across Brandon's face disarmed me.

'It's beautiful, Andrew,' he said. 'Having the key so close to the lock makes the torment even more delicate, more delicious.'

I wasn't sure.

I was uneasy again. I'd known Brandon, like Donaldson, as a respectable academic. I hadn't seen the private side of the man. We'd met once or twice a year to talk about each others' students. We would act as external examiners for one another. It was a good arrangement. Our respective departments liked it too. We were far enough apart not to have day-to-day contact, but close enough to avoid the costs of overnight stays for meetings.

'You didn't wear that under a suit, did you?' I said. I hadn't intended being quite so direct.

Brandon smiled.

'I didn't then,' he said. 'But I do now, quite often in fact. A few people know. Others think that I'm supplementing my pension, keeping my academic hand in, if you will, as my Master's research assistant. Well, I can't do quite as much around the house and yard as I once did, but, it's a great way of life. Since Marshall, my partner died, I saw no reason to stay in Seattle.'

I shook my head. I hadn't even appreciated that Brandon was gay.

I'd admired and respected him, you know, but from a distance. We'd had our differences.

We had a great home, nice friends, he was saying, on campus and at the church. We enjoyed the theater and the symphony, we were always there. This part of me became a little easier to express as Marshall got older. We'd no longer go on for drinks afterwards. I'd take him home, see him into bed and then change into leather and head for the Eagle.

Eldon saw me there, of course. He'd been up to the house, with all the other students in the group at Christmastime. Marshall and I saw no reason to hide ourselves away, so usually twice a year, we would invite our tutorial groups around for drinks. Those were pleasant occasions. The freshmen could be slightly uncomfortable, especially if it was the first time they'd come across two middle-aged men living together. By the time they were ready to move on, many of them had become good friends. I think Eldon was the only student I knew in all my years there who was a regular at the Eagle before he got his degree.

I saw a studious young man in him. He would work hard and play hard. He wrestled for the college. He was good. He helped me with Marshall too. He'd come and take him out in his chair when it became too much for him to walk. He'd come and stay at the house if I had to go away for a few days. Eldon stayed in our house when I took Marshall to Florida, the summer before he died, to see his daughter and sister. Eldon was the one who held my hand through all the funeral arrangements. I'd known Marshall was dying, but I'd become so involved in the day-to-day arrangements of making sure he could live as full a life as possible, that I wasn't prepared for a sudden end. He'd gone to get a bottle of wine for dinner. He could get around quite quickly in the chair on his own. I heard him open the closet we used as a wine cellar, and call me. By the time I'd got there he was dead.

I was still sitting there, on the floor beside him, holding his hand and crying my heart out when Eldon arrived. He had his own key by then. He was the one who took charge, who gave me a drink and sat me down, who called the doctor. He was the one who found the burned out pan in the kitchen just in time to prevent a fire.'

We were sitting quietly together by that time. We watched the others as they made good use of Donaldson's gym.

Eldon stayed with me for a while. I wrote his reference to get him a place here, said Brandon, smiling as he relived the memory. I was so proud when he finally got tenure, but I felt very alone when he'd gone. The Washington house had been great for two of us, or more; Marshall and I often had visitors. It felt very empty when he wasn't there any more and no one visited.

I advertised for roommates, but, well, you know, the age difference, it was too much. I didn't like their music or their untidiness. They were shocked by this old man dressing up in leather, or wearing only shorts around the house. It didn't seem to be working. I tried writing. I found I'd start something then spend hours just gazing out of the window, I was not happy.

It was Donaldson who rescued me. We hadn't known about each other until we met at the Eagle one night, many years ago, probably before I'd met Eldon. Donaldson was in Seattle to give a lecture I think and had arranged to see someone. He was smart like that, mixing pleasure and business, especially when someone else is paying for the air ticket and hotel. He had a young man in tow, literally, on a collar and chain, when we saw each other. I'd made a remark about the young man. It had been enough to get us talking. We hadn't needed to say anything about our interests. They were accepted, respected. We met for dinner the next night and, by dessert, we'd become great friends. After that, he always stayed with us when he was visiting the area. He'd try and get to see us at least once or twice a year.

He'd wanted to come out especially for Marshall's funeral, but he'd had to go to Europe. He was cross about that. Marshall's interest in native American history sat well alongside Donaldson's knowledge of anthropology. They could talk each other through the night and through many a bottle of whiskey.

It was what, probably a month or so later, when he called and said he'd be in town. It was sudden, the following day. Did I mind the short notice? Of course I didn't, I was grateful for the company. I drove out to the airport to meet him. I chauffeured him around town that day. I'd sit and wait in the car, reading, or listen to classical music on the local NPR station as he had his meetings. I had nothing else to do and, truth be told, I was really glad of having something that kept me away from the house for a few hours. Donaldson was tired though.

He took me to dinner. As I was driving, he had drunk most of a bottle of wine before suggesting that we went on to the Eagle.

He called me from the study after breakfast the following morning. He'd had an e-mail about a run in San Francisco. I remember the conversation to this day. He'd printed off the details and let me read them.

We've never played, Brandon,' Donaldson had said, but if you'd like to come along, I'd be more than pleased if you'd be my guest. You've been my host here so often. There's no obligation. You can do as much as you want, or as little, just sit in the Californian sunshine and watch the perverts play, if you like.

I'd been a little embarrassed by his candor. I'd said nothing until dinner that night.

Thank you, I'd said, I'd like to accept your invitation to the run.

Donaldson had been so pleased. He was taking a risk, inviting a relative novice but, we'd talked more about it as we ate, and as we enjoyed some whiskey afterwards. Donaldson seems to be able to identify guys' inner needs, before they do themselves, it's a skill he's never lost. I was a little scared at the thought of some of the heavier play, but, as Donaldson said, I didn't have to join in if I didn't want to.

When he was due to leave, the following morning, I wouldn't let him call a cab. I insisted on driving him to the airport, even though it was the rush hour. He'd been on the phone, so I'd carried his bag out to the car. When he came out of the house, the back door of the car was open. Until then, he'd always sat in the front beside me.

Perhaps he wasn't thinking, any way, I didn't say anything. Having seen him with the young man at the Eagle, I smiled. I closed the door, got in and drove. I could see him in the mirror as I steered the car through the traffic. He was engrossed in his papers and then the morning newspaper.

It wasn't until I drove into the airport parking lot that he noticed what had happened. He was desperately apologetic, saying how sorry he was for the rudeness, for taking me for granted. I smiled and said nothing as I walked with him, carrying his case to the check-in. The parting was formal. He was in a business suit, carrying his briefcase. I was a little more casual, in khaki pants, but wearing a tie. We shook hands, but there was a knowing grin on both our faces.

I was woken by the FedEx delivery man the next morning.

I wondered what the square box could be. I was about to refuse to sign for it, but I saw Donaldson's name as the sender. I almost tore the box from the man's hands then. I was disheveled, unshaven, wearing only some cotton boxer shorts. I must have looked a sight. I didn't even take any notice of the delivery man.

I stopped dead still when I first saw what was in the box. Then I laughed. I laughed and I laughed and I laughed, said Brandon.

I was puzzled. What was Brandon talking about?

'It was a hat, Andrew,' he explained, 'a gray peaked chauffeur's hat. I still have it. I wear it for Eldon.'

I nodded.

'I know,' I said, 'I saw you arrive.'

He smiled, then went on with his tale. I nearly took the to California with me, to the run, he said, but I didn't trust myself not to lose it or damage it. I'd got there early and had been helping the organizers when Donaldson arrived. I kissed him for the first time that day, to say thank you, both for the hat and for rescuing my sanity. He'd just grinned, held my hand for a moment and said nothing. You know what he can be like.

The run was amazing. There was so much going on. We were staying in tents, somewhere not far from Russian River. I'd met one of the organizers in San Francisco and he'd driven me there.

That first evening, I watched as a young man was bent over a frame and paddled. I was told afterwards that it had taken him five years to develop sufficient confidence to let one of the West Coast's most renowned paddlers work on him. I saw a young man, beautiful in his youth, walking around behind an older man. The young man was chained, shackled, his hands behind his back, clanking with every step he took. They puzzled me. The young man looked as if he was somewhere else. There was something almost hypnotic about his expression. The older man seemed to be showing him off, as if saying I'm fat, and middle-aged, but I can still have a pretty young man like this on a lead. It worried me.

There was so much there. I didn't know what I wanted to do. I was scared too. I enjoyed providing service for someone, but I wasn't sure about how I would react to some of the sensations. Yet, there they were, all these men, half my age, some a third, walking round with what they called 'hamburger backs'. It didn't seem to be doing them any real, lasting, physical harm. I'd read about the violence, but there didn't seem to be any there. There was always someone looking on, checking that everything was alright, safe, consentual, even when a bullwhip was hitting someone's shoulder blades and blood was running down their back. I could see the grin, the achievement, the satisfaction and achievement on a man's face.

I had a tent on my own that first night. Another man was expected, but not until the next day. He'd arrived when I'd been out, away. I'd gone back for something, I can't remember what, it doesn't matter. I'd found a leather jacket lying there. It had seemed natural to pick it up and put it on a hanger. There were boots left untidily and jeans. I folded them all neatly and put them carefully to one side. I hoped my compatriot wasn't going to be too messy.

I didn't discover who it was until that night. I'd come and gone and seen more clothing left out and about. I'd tidied up each time I'd gone back. After dinner, I'd gone into the woods. I'd watched as one man had been tied to a bench and spirit on his back had been set alight. I'd seen another tied upside down and hung from the branch of a tree. The bondage must have taken two guys the best part of an hour. It was, I was told the next day, after dawn when he was finally let down and untied.

I got back to the tent to find someone else there. I could see boots and black leather pants. The rest of the man was in shadow. I started to speak, but heard only a 'sshh' sound. I shut up. I said nothing and crawled into my sleeping bag. I wondered how this strange man was. I hoped if he was going to be so rude that I'd see him as little as possible.

I hadn't realized just quite what I was wishing myself in to. I must have been tired, because I fell asleep quite quickly. The last I remember seeing was this man's calves in the tight black leather. They looked good. I felt a stirring in my cock, but I was too tired to do anything about it, and apart from which I didn't think it would be a particularly good idea to disturb my neighbor again.

I got my surprise when I woke. I came to, aware that I could not move my hands or feet and that I could feel the air against my naked skin. I tried to see. I could open my eyes, but there was still darkness. I tried to shout, but my mouth was full. It took me a few moments to realize that I had been bound and gagged and was blindfold too. I tried to move, but my struggles were useless. Both my hands and feet had been anchored securely.

I was even more surprised when a voice, very close to my ear, told me to relax and enjoy it. I thought I recognized the voice. I was still sleepy. It wasn't Donaldson, I knew that much. I tried to work out who it could be. I was confused. I didn't recall the voice as having been one of the others on the run I'd met the previous day.

I was still trying to run through the possibilities when I felt his hands starting to massage me gently. His fingertips ran up my stomach and chest. I could feel my cock hardening. There was something very special about the moment. I was there, tied, bound, helpless, erect, excited with a man I didn't know. I felt him kiss me gently on the cheek. This wasn't the action of the storybooks. This was too romantic, too sensuous. Those written tales were violent.

I was confused. New sensations were hitting my brain, hard and fast. I was aware of something pinching my nipples. I could feel the intensity growing. I felt something warm and soothing across my stomach and around my cock and balls. It took me a few moments to realize that I was being shaved. The fresh morning air felt alien but divine on the unguarded skin. I could feel my erection bobbing with excitement.

I could feel a body close to mine. It felt naked too. I tried to lift my head forward, but without success, as the gag was taken from my mouth. An intense masculine aroma hit my nostrils a second before the flesh touched my lips. I put out my tongue and started to lick. It took me a few moments before I understood what I was doing. I was licking the man's balls. I applied myself hard but gently. I'd seen men the day before hitting each other's balls with mallets, hanging large weights from their sacs or squeezing their testicles in vices. I'd seen others, the observers, cupping themselves protectively, pained by even the thought of such intensity. I wondered whether I should chew this man's balls or not. I didn't get a chance. He'd been squatting over me. I could feel him rub his cock along my lips. It was hard, full, thick and long. Without thinking, I kissed the tip. There was a taste of piss at the slit. I felt a hand ruffle my hair. I felt another playing with my cock, tapping it from side to side.

I was so excited that I didn't notice for a few moments that the man was no longer there. I found I could move my hands and feet.

I reached up and pushed the blindfold away. I blinked hard in the bright morning sunshine. It took me a few seconds to see that I was on the ground outside the tent. There were two tent pegs marking where my hands and feet had been tied. I looked around. There was, I thought for an instant, no one there.

It took me a few minutes to appreciate fully where I was. I sat up and rubbed my wrists, my arms and my ankles. I wondered where my tormentor had gone.

It must have been a full five minutes before I saw the piece of paper and the boots in the tent entrance.

The words had come from a computer; there was no handwriting as a clue. There was just one sentence: 'If you'd like to try being my slave for the next two days, then all you have to do is kiss each of these boots and then replace the blindfold, kneel and wait for your Master.'

I was so excited by that time that I didn't need any more persuading. I crawled on to my hands and knees, found the blindfold and moved forward. I kissed those boots, first the left, then the right, before depriving myself of my sight. I knelt back on my haunches.

I could hear the zip on the tent opening. A pair of hands lifted mine from my sides. They let me run my hands down the sides of tight fitting leather pants. I felt the butt too. It was round and firm. I heard another zip and then the head of the cock touched my lips again. Instinctively, I opened my mouth. A hand went under my chin and pushed my jaw shut. The cockhead rested against my lips.

It was hard.

I felt the cockhead being pulled away. I felt a man's face approaching mine. I could feel his breath on my cheeks and smell toothpaste as he exhaled. I felt my hands being pushed behind my back. The lips touched mine. Even though I was blindfold, I had my eyes closed. The leather covering was pushed back. The lips were still touching me. I opened my eyes. It was Eldon.

I was so shocked that I threw my arms around his butt and hugged him. The leather felt good against his butt. I looked him up and down. He'd put his cock away and the leather pants were closed once more. If he was surprised by my reaction, Eldon never showed it. I started to move, but his expression told me not to. Instinctively, I remained silent. I should, I knew, speak only when spoken to. I didn't know it then, but my entire existence had changed.

I stayed kneeling as Eldon went back into the tent. I looked round. I could see no one else. I had no means of knowing even the time, but inside I knew that I didn't really need to know. I was enjoying an unfamiliar inner peace when Eldon returned. He had a black leather collar in his hand. I lifted myself from my haunches and bowed my head. I knew exactly where that collar was going. It only took a few moments. I hadn't looked closely at the collar. I had expected that it would have a standard buckle fastening. It didn't. I felt the pressure on my neck for a few moments as a lock was snapped in to place. I could also feel my cock, standing out hard, in the morning air. I bent forward and kissed each of Eldon's boots, as gracefully as I could. It was the best way, the only way, I could thank him.

Eldon noticed my erection. He prodded it with his foot. I felt I should have been embarrassed, being naked and erect in such a predicament. Instead, I felt calm. Eldon handed me some shorts and pointed to my boots. I stood. I couldn't say that with so little that I got dressed, but the baggy cotton shorts did a little to conceal my excitement. I stayed a pace behind the young man as we walked towards the compound where meals were served. He hadn't said anything, but I found myself remembering what I'd see other guys doing the previous day.

Eldon collected his own breakfast, but silently expected me to fetch his coffee. I sat down on the ground beside him. He rubbed my head. I knew that I went red when Donaldson saw me. I was disarmed when he blew me a kiss and rubbed his hands. It was reassuring. Although I was tense and excited, Donaldson's gesture made me laugh. I smiled.

I stayed with Eldon, beside him, throughout the long weekend. I'd carry and fetch for him. I sat quietly in the shade cleaning his boots. I looked after his leather and kept our tent neat and tidy. He showed me a box that contained the tools and toys that he used. He instructed me how to clean each item and how it should be stored. He told me what foods he liked and did not like, how his coffee should be fixed, the brands of beer and whiskey that he drank. I wanted a notebook, but all I had was my concentration.

When we got back to the tent after breakfast, he took away almost everything I'd brought with me. He locked all my possessions, except my boots, in his car. I was permitted my toothbrush, razor, a towel and my boots. Eldon certainly knew what he was doing. He allowed me shorts or swimbriefs during the day. After that first morning, he set a routine. I was permitted to lick his body then. I started with his feet and worked slowly to his neck. Only then was I permitted to kiss each of his balls and slowly up his cock. I also had to kiss each foot and the narrow band of flesh between his balls and his hole. I'd be hard as soon as I started this daily ritual, but all that was allowed to touch my cock was his flesh when I brushed it accidentally.

At that point, he'd take my collar off and send me to shower. He didn't say anything, but I shaved my body too each time. I'm not a hairy man, but I made sure that there was not even stubble around my cock and balls. Eldon noticed that on the second day, how a patch of hair that he had missed when he'd shaved me for the first time had gone. He gave me calamine lotion to rub in too. It stopped razor rash, he said. Then, I would kneel, ready for him to replace the collar and lock it for a new day. Just as I had done that first morning, I would bend and thank him.

Eldon had me do a lot of watching over that weekend. On the Sunday afternoon, he said we should talk. We stayed by our tent, away from the others.

He sat on a box. I knelt on the ground. He'd only spoken once.

'Tell me,' Eldon had said, 'what you are thinking.'

It came out without any structure. It was a little like praying, trying to find the words to say what you want. Simply having to express my thoughts helped me sort them out. I was, I told Eldon, feeling exceedingly fulfilled. I had found a peace. It felt right to be doing what I was doing. I wasn't, I told him, sure about how much pain I could take. I still found it hard to understand how some guys seemed to get so much pleasure from accepting such intense and severe stimulation.

I wasn't into punishment either, I told him. I wanted to do what I was going as a way of helping him, of giving him a part of me. I wanted to do what I was doing well, with pride. I preferred, I told him, the reassurance of being told something had been done well. If a task wasn't done well enough, silence would tell me all I needed to know.

Eldon said very little. He listened though, attentively. He nodded, encouraging me to say more. I brought him up to date with my life since Rob had died and the emptiness of it all. I told him about Donaldson's invitation, about trips to the Eagle where I would stand around, dressed in leather, and talk to people, but never do anything. I never really had,

I admitted. It had seemed wrong to want, to try, to do too much when Rob was alive. We'd agreed to be faithful to one another twenty years earlier. I felt that even sucking another man's cock would have betrayed him. We hadn't talked about it, but Rob knew as his illness became more serious that I wasn't doing anything. He called out to me one night, when I'd come back from the Eagle, that he wouldn't mind if I brought someone home. I knew I couldn't, not then. It still seemed wrong to take someone back to our home just for sex which would be ephemeral and fleeting.

I could see Eldon thinking as I spoke. I didn't know what was on his mind. I looked him up and down. He looked good. He was wearing only a tanktop with his leather jeans and boots. The muscles of his arms, shoulders and chest were tanned and firmly defined. I could see his abdominals, outlined under the tight cotton. The leather framed the solidity of his thighs. I'd always noticed good looking men, but that weekend, my perceptions had sharpened. I had watched as one Master had put two slaves through a fierce workout. Apparently, there had been arguments at previous events, complaints even, that there were no weights or workout facilities. This time, the organizers had made sure they were provided.

I'd watched, carefully, as the Master had supervised the young men, making them kiss his boots with every push-up, his legs with every crunch, how he had made sure that each repetition had been done exactly and precisely. It had been an awesome performance. The young men, dressed only in jockstraps, had been sweating profusely within seconds, but they had kept up their efforts and exertion for more than an hour. I had been impressed. I had been jealous too, I think. I had felt my cock hardening inside the shorts I'd been allowed to wear at the time.

Eventually, Eldon had spoken.

'Would you,' he asked, 'like to come east for the summer?'

It took me no time to answer.

'Yes, Sir,' I said.

'In which case,' he said, bending forward and kissing me on the forehead, 'we have some work to do.'

I followed as we set off toward the compound where the weights were. Two men were working out. Once I recognized as the run physician. He was an older guy, in his sixties. He too was in excellent shape. He was gray and his hair had been left at a length that could best be described as conventionally respectable. He didn't seem in the least surprised when Eldon and I arrived. The other, a younger man, was in equally good shape.

'This,' Eldon said, 'is Doctor Mulhouse.'

I nodded respectfully. I didn't think offering a hand was appropriate protocol.

'He's going to give you a thorough physical,' Eldon said.

He'd disappeared before I had a chance to respond. It was only then that the Doctor offered me his hand.

'And, this is Philip,' he said, looking at the young man, 'he's a nurse who works in my office in Chicago.'

It must have taken the best part of two hours for the Doctor to go through the examination. I was measured, weighed, I had to run on the treadmill, lift some weights, I had my blood pressure measured, several times, my pulse taken and my heart monitored. I sat on the ground and answered a comprehensive questionnaire. I signed a form authorizing the Doctor to request copies of my medical records. He took blood. I pissed in a pot. He stuck a finger in my ass. I'd felt a little awkward at first.

It was Philip who opened my eyes.

'Eldon must sure think a lot of you if he's going to all this trouble,' he said as he pulled my shorts down, ready for the

Doctor to examine my cock and balls. I smiled then. I hadn't thought of it that way. I was glowing with pride when I finally made my way back to our tent.

Eldon was there, waiting. A rubber bottle was hanging upside down from the tent post, a tube running from it. He gave me no time. He pulled my shorts off and put me in a position with my head on the ground and my butt in the air. I was surprised by the gentleness and care with which he opened my hole, lubricated it and fed in the tube. I remained still, savoring the new sensation as liquid ran into me. I could feel a pressure on my belly. It was unfamiliar, a little uncomfortable, but not painful, at least not then.

He let me rest for a few moments when the bottle was empty. Then, he lifted my head and pulled me gently to my feet. Eldon was a man of few words. He pushed me down so that I squatted. That's when I could feel the pressure, the intensity of the liquid in my ass. I could tell from his expression that I was not to spill any.

I was tensing my hands, holding my eyes closed and concentrating hard to keep my ass closed when he spoke.

'Go over there,' he said, pointing to a tree about thirty yards away, 'squat and let it all out. You can come back when you think you're empty.'

I was embarrassed then. I noticed that a small hole had been dug beside the tree. I did as I was told. I could feel my face relax as I let go and a torrent of liquid shot out of my ass. I tried not to force the muscles, but let the liquid drain out. A few times I thought that I was empty, there'd then be a gurgle and a few drops more would dribble out of me.

I'd watched Eldon while this was happening. He'd seen I'd squatted and then almost ignored me. He'd put a couple of tent pegs into the ground and brought some rope from his box. He'd also brought out a pillow from the tent.

I walked slowly back when I felt sure I was empty. Eldon indicated that I should lie on the ground. Slowly and carefully, he bound rope around each of my wrists. I closed my eyes and relished the sensations as he did. I opened them again, briefly, when he started to wind rope around each of my knees. He pulled my legs back then, tying my knees to the tent pegs too. My thighs were tight against my chest, my ass open to the air. Eldon pushed the pillow under the small of my back. I tried to lift my head, to try to watch as he disappeared into the tent.

I closed my eyes. I tried to move my wrists, but the bondage was too firm. It wasn't in any way uncomfortable, Eldon had secured my hands so well, and there was no rubbing under my knees. There was nothing I could do but appreciate the situation. I could feel my cock hardening and my balls drawing themselves up against me in the afternoon sunshine.

I didn't see Eldon come out of the tent. I was so far away in my thoughts that I didn't notice him until I felt him brush against my ass. When I opened my eyes, suddenly, blinking against the bright sunshine, I saw him there, kneeling against me. I tried to raise my head to see more, but the way he had tied my knees also kept my shoulders firmly against the ground.

He reached forward and put a hand over my mouth. I took a deep breath. I knew now what was happening. I felt every fraction of an inch as Eldon's thick cock penetrated me that first time. He did it so gently. I could feel my muscle being stretched and I could feel my eyes widening, my mouth opening and the smile of delight breaking across my face. My mouth was dry when his lips touched mine. I tried to reach forward for him, but he'd pulled back.

Eldon made love to me that afternoon, claiming me as his

own. He filled me with his cock, as far as it would go and then held himself hard and firm against me, not moving an inch as my mouth sucked strongly on his tongue, licked his face and tasted the stubble on his chin. The smell from Eldon's body got stronger, yet he kept himself still. I could feel his erection, deep within me. I tried to give Eldon pleasure. I tried to tense and relax the muscles of my ass on his hard cock. I wanted to give him everything, to save him from having to work.

He started to pump me eventually. It was very gently at first. He'd pull back, almost until he had come out of me, leaving only the head of his cock in contact with my muscle. Then, he would very slowly come back into me, until I could feel the bone of his pelvis pressing against my balls, squeezing them where they were lying. It was more as if he was trying to do that than fuck me for a while.

Then, slowly, gradually, before I had really appreciated what he was doing, the speed and intensity of his thrusts was increasing. I could feel the head of his thick, long cock, jabbing against my prostate.

I could feel the tension growing in my hands and face. When Eldon brought his mouth against mine, I pulled on his tongue, sucking hard as if it was a cock.

Eldon built up an intensity several times. I would start to brace myself, trying to prepare my body and mind for the power that I knew would come with his orgasm when he would slow down and relax a little. I'd open my eyes and he'd look down, grin, and smile at me, teasing me. I wished my arms were free then; I wanted to hug him, embrace him and thank him for permitting me to provide him with such service and pleasure.

I'd relaxed and had my head back, taking deep breaths when he attacked me. I thought he would re-enter me as gently as he had each previous time when he had slowly pulled back. It was the first and only time I made that mistake. He drove into me with such power that I felt as if my whole body was moving against the rough ground. My eyes and mouth flew open. I saw his sadistic grin before he leaned forward and kissed me on the lips. We both knew. Nothing had to be said.

I don't know how many thrusts he made, but I knew he was cumming. I wanted to keep my eyes closed, to feel every minute sensation, but I wanted to see him too. I opened my eyes. His eyes were closed now. I looked at the beauty that was the definition in his biceps as he held his weight. I saw the ripples in his stomach muscles as he moved his pelvis backwards and forwards. I saw his mouth start to open.

The shout when it came was so loud birds flew out of nearby trees. I fought hard to concentrate, to squeeze my muscle, to provide him with pleasure as long as I could. He fell against me, his weight pressing my legs against my chest. He kissed me again. He stayed inside me for a long time. I thought at one moment that he might have fallen asleep. He hadn't. Even then, he could read me. He gently tapped my shoulder to let me know he was okay. I relaxed again then.

I licked the sweat from his forehead. It tasted so good. I was happy, happier than I had been in a very long time.

'Brandon's story helped me too.'

Andrew was speaking for himself again now.

"I understood what he had been through and what he had achieved.'

I let him think, not wanting to divert his train of thought.

'Oh, yes,' he added, 'although I didn't know it that day, I met my mentor for the training Luke had arranged: Coach Benini. Luke didn't tell me it was Mr Benini. I found out the following weekend. My time with Coach Benini was quite something too, but that's a story for another day.'

I was left curious. Andrew smiled, kissed me and then disappeared.

He went to assist his Master. I went to sit and think.

Andrew's acceptance

'Yes, I know,' Andrew said when we met again the following day. 'You're curious to know how I came from being Donaldon's guest to being Lord Cunningham's slave.'

I nodded.

Curiosity had got the better of me. In more than ten years of going to the runs, only once – in September 2001 – had I let the distraction of the world outside the site intrude.

Usually, the deal with my roommates was that the television and radio would stay off. There would be no newspapers. As news junkies, the isolation was about the only time each year that we had to detox. As technology had intruded, we'd also agreed that laptops and cellphones would only be used for work emergencies.

I broke that promise.

I booted my laptop and logged on. I wanted to know more about Amos, Lord Cunningham.

The search engines did their work. I found out about his Navy career, his success in business, rising to be chief executive of one of the biggest banks and investment companies in the City of London, his patronage of the arts and architecture; the bank's new headquarters building had become a feature of the London skyline before it was even completed and had won its acclaimed designer several more prestigious awards.

I found out his marriage, how he had become estranged

from Sarah, Lady Lawnswood, but they had never divorced. I read about his three adult children, about the son who had followed him into finance and the daughter who was one of the fastest-rising women in the Royal Navy. There was nothing about the youngest son since he had started Eton, about fifteen years earlier. I'd explore my morbid curiosity about the traditions of aristocratic younger sons and check *Crockfords' Clerical Dictionary* to see if the third son, imaginatively called Tertius, had ended up in the Church when I had more time. There were diary and social column mentions of course as well as the business reports, the speeches to industry conferences and contributions to each February's World Economic Forum in Davos, Switzerland. Nothing was even remotely salacious. There were elegant women on Sir Amos's arm in the Royal Enclosure at Ascot, in the Royal Box at Covent Garden.

Some commentators had accused him of political cronyism when – at fifty-five – he'd handed over control of the bank to a younger man, accepting the position of chairman to go with his elevation to the House of Lords. Unlike many, he rejected party allegiances to sit on the cross benches as an independent.

I saw Andrew with him in a photograph taken shortly after this. Lord Cunningham had been commissioned by the UK government to investigate and report on the funding of pharmaceutical research. His inquiry had brought him to the industry's US heartlands, to New Jersey and Research Triangle near Raleigh in South Carolina. He'd been to the Ivy League universities too, to Yale, Harvard, Princeton, to Columbia in New York City and to the industry lobbyists in DC.

There, at a black-tie fund-raiser, were His Lordship, Donaldson and Andrew.

'I have some of the picture,' I told Andrew when we got to speak again. 'I did some research.'

'Perhaps you know more than I do?' he said when I told him what I'd found. 'I hadn't realized pictures of that gala evening were online. I suppose I should have done, but you don't always think about it, do you?'

'So?' I asked. 'What happened?'

Well, said Andrew as he picked up one of His Lordship's Dehner patrol boots and lovingly started to add to the already mirror-like polish, Donaldson had met the Master at one of the hearings for that inquiry. It could have been in DC, New York or Princeton. They're all within easy reach. I think Donaldson had done what he usually does; he invited His Lordship to visit.

It must have been for a weekend, between hearings or meetings. I know when he arrived in Pennsylvania he was just so grateful to have some time in the comfort of a home, rather than yet another hotel room. Yes, he probably was staying in places far more grand and expensive than even well-paid academics or even pharmaceutical consultants can afford, but even the best hotels are still hotels.

I don't think Donaldson knew the Master that intimately then. I think he'd noticed that His Lordship was tired and tense. I'd been to Donaldson's a few times by then. He'd arranged for me to spend time with men he knew, men from whom I could learn, some of them are here, by the way, but I liked going back there. I got on really well with Luke; he'd become like a younger brother to me, the younger brother I'd never had, and a mentor too. I was learning so much from him, and having the time to swim and work out every day, that was great too.

Donaldson ordered us to be more discrete than usual. Nakedness was banned. We could wear shorts around the house, and tanktops, but the shorts had to be knee-length and baggy.

I think we'd even put on shirts and chinos to serve dinner on the Friday evening after His Lordship had arrived. There was a panic when he asked for pink gin. I'd had to rush to the store to try to find Angustura bitters. He was happy then.

Everything changed on the Saturday morning. Luke had served breakfast on the deck. His Lordship was sitting, reading The Financial Times and Wall Street Journal, a cup of coffee beside him when I came out of the house. His Lordship saw me as I was heading for the gym in the barn. He asked where I was going. I told him. I hadn't finished speaking before he was beside me.

I don't think anyone of us had thought that Lord Cunningham would want to use the gym. We'd expected him to appreciate the pool, but not to workout for some reason.

I'd been relatively conventional. I'd put running shorts on over my jock, at least to get to the barn building. I was thinking that, once I'd shut the door, I would get rid of the shorts.

'Just do what you usually do,' His Lordship had said when we got there.

I did. He'd wandered around, looking at the equipment, picking up a light weight here, and pulling a handle there. I was busy. I'd done some dumbbell presses; I didn't like to do bench presses without someone to spot, and I didn't feel it right to ask a guest to do that. I'd done some pulldowns and I was just moving on to some curls when His Lordship's question stopped me.

'Andrew,' he said. I was pleasantly surprised that he'd remembered my name. 'Is that what I think it is?'

He was looking directly at the squats bench. A dildo was

fixed in place, standing proudly upright, waiting for the next user. Just to make sure I couldn't avoid the question, he pointed.

'Yes, Sir,' I answered. 'It probably is.'

I remember the smile spreading across his face. "You use it?'

'Yes, Sir, I do.' I said. I couldn't really have denied it. Donaldson had always advocated honesty too. Apart from which, my subservient place in the household – like Luke's – had been totally obvious from the moment that His Lordship had arrived the previous evening.

I waited for His Lordship's reaction. I stood there in silence. Somehow I expected him to disapprove, after all, he was a pillar of the establishment figure, someone close to government, to power. He had important friends.

I still wasn't quite sure to make of what was happening as he walked towards the bench. He reached down and felt the dildo.

'A nice size,' he said I hadn't expected him to know anything about dildos, let alone appreciate their sizes. 'Aren't you going to show me?'

I think my surprise must really have shown then.

'Good God man,' he said. 'How naive do you think I am?'

I didn't know how to respond to that, so I made my way to the bench. I opened the locker and took out the pot of lube with my name on it. I could see His Lordship loosening up as I took off the shorts and pushed some lube into my hole. I put some onto the dildo too.

'Douched ready?' he asked.

'Yes, Sir,' I said. 'I always do before a workout.'

His knowledge was no longer surprising me, it was intriguing me. Deference, and my position, stopped me from asking him questions.

I moved the dumbbells into position. His Lordship approached. He handed me them one at a time, so I didn't have to move my position over the dildo.

'How many do you usually do?'

'Three sets of ten, Sir,' I answered.

'Do them.'

I positioned myself over the dildo. I could feel it pressing against my hole. The weights were heavy in my hands. I concentrated, willing the sphincter to relax as I bent my knees. I closed my eyes. I'd really learned to appreciate and enjoy my hole being worked. I groaned as the rubber went into me.

I took the sets slowly, appreciating and savoring every thrust. After ten, I waited, getting my breath back with the dildo still an inch or so inside me. I did the same after the second set.

'That was good.'

I opened my eyes when I heard the words of encouragement. His Lordship was sitting on one of the other benches. I looked across at him. The erection in his pants was clearly visible.

'Perhaps you should do more?' he suggested.

I bent, letting the dildo into me as far as I could. I rested, then slowly raised my body to the vertical again. The dildo inside me felt so good. I didn't really want to let it out. I moved up and down on it a few times. I heard His Lordship groan with appreciation. I tried to bring the penetration and my breathing together, letting the dildo push my diaphragm upwards. I inhaled as I straightened my knees, letting the dildo out. I kept going, letting the piece of rubber gently fuck me. The sensation was exquisite.

'Nice ass too,' he said. 'I like a nice ass.'

I was really in a dilemma now. Donaldson had said

nothing about intimacy and Lord Cunningham, let alone service or submission. Part of me felt I should go, offer myself to him, put him out of his misery, or at least relieve his frustration. Another part of me felt an obligation, even though nothing had even been said, let alone formalized, towards Donaldson.

His Lordship stood up and walked slowly towards me.

'A few more, please,' he said.

I did. I was trying to make the descents onto the dildo as slow and sensuous as I could, putting on the best show that I was able, when the barn door opened. I opened my eyes when the extra light became apparent.

'So this is where you are.'

It was Donaldson.

His Lordship was immediately all courtesy.

'Donaldson, my friend, you don't mind I hope? I was taking advantage of your man, encouraging to put on a display for me.'

'Not in the least, Your Lordship. I'm delighted he's providing you with some stimulation.'

Donaldson caught my eye. There was a determination, a dominance in his expression that I'd seen directed at Luke, but I'd never experienced myself. His Lordship was looking at me. So too was Donaldson. I stood, the dildo a few inches into my hole as Donaldson's eyes gave me the instructions that I'd been hoping for, and which I've never regretted.

Donaldson's eyes were directed at His Lordship's fly, even though Donaldson was behind him, I knew where he was pointing. I nodded as discretely as I could. My head can't have moved more than a fraction of an inch. It was the re-assurance Donaldson wanted too.

Donaldson smiled. I could see him trying to think of the most delicious words he could use.

'Well then,' he said. 'if it pleases Your Lordship ...'

The laughter started as he turned away from me towards Donaldson. He was chuckling as his gaze met Donaldson's.

'Yes?' he asked, 'if what pleases me?'

Donaldson was grinning too. In that fraction of a second, the two men had achieved an understanding and an intimacy that has lasted until this day.

'I think, Your Lordship,' Donaldson teased, 'that it will be Andrew who may please you. He's reasonably trained now. Use him as you will.'

Lord Cunningham didn't even have time to express his thanks before Donaldson was gone.

I was just starting to appreciate what he'd said as the door closed behind him.

* * *

'Stand up, turn round and bend forward.'

The tone of His Lordship's instruction startled me. He was the officer again, as well as being the gentleman. I obeyed. I knew I didn't have any choice. My cock started hardening inside my jockstrap. I'd been enjoying the dildo fuck too much to think about it. Now, the dominance had lit a different response.

I could just see as His Lordship reached for one of the condoms in the locker. He was opening the packet as he positioned himself behind me. I could feel more than see as he undid his fly and pushed his pants down his thighs. I could feel his hands against my butt as he pulled the condom into place.

I'd just caught my breath as he entered me. The thrust was almost violent, animal-like. If I hadn't consented, this would have been rape at its most viscious. His Lordship was hung too. I felt the air pushed out of me. I could feel my eyes being pushed out of their sockets too. Wow, I thought. I felt the pressure on my prostate, the stretch of my sphincter. I was relieved I'd had a chance to open up using the dildo. "That fuck didn't last long. It was an action of necessity, far past the threshold of desire. It was bestial. I grasped the bench to hold my position as this man thrust into me again and again. His Lordship grasped my hips tightly, keeping me still as he pounded my hole. I could feel the sharpness of his nails digging further and further in as his climax approached.

'Yes!' The shout was like a sportsman, releasing days, weeks, of pent-up energy in a triumphant, all-conquering victory. His Lordship's hands left my thighs. They were in the air, clenched, his biceps, every muscle of his body tense then relaxing as his cum filled the condom inside me.

I could feel his eyes closing, his head going back, his muscles starting to relax as he relished the glory of his orgasm. I squeezed the mighty cock in my ass as gently as I could, slowly tensing then relaxing my sphincter.

I heard him chuckle. I continued squeezing, trying to pull the huge cock as deep within me as I could.

I was still squeezing when his body relaxed against me. I could feel the warmth of his thighs. I was sorry that his shirt was between his chest and my back. I wanted to feel his skin against mine.

I was caught unawares when he graced the back of my neck with his lips. He kissed me, as sweetly as I have ever been kissed, in the hollow behind the lobe of my left ear.

'Yee.... aaaa .....'

The scream started deep in my stomach. I felt myself pulling His Lordship's cock further into me. I'd forgotten about my own dick, trapped within the jockstrap. I let go of the bench, my arms started to move upwards as the orgasm became more intense.

His Lordship saw what was happening. He pulled the jock forward and put his hand at the end of my cock. He caught the cum as I shot. My arms were out, diagonally, when the ejaculation erupted.

'Yes, yes, yes.' I pulled air in through my clenched teeth. 'Yes, Sir!'

My fingers were curling as the orgasm started to subside. My mouth fell open. Instinctively, I started licking when I felt His Lordship's hand reach my lips. I couldn't remember when I'd last cum. I couldn't remember either when I'd last tasted my own cum.

I was at that point where an orgasm has left the physical, to become the spiritual. My head was moving, slowly, from side to side. I shook it, trying to bring my eyes back into focus. Despite the raw vigor of the fuck, I felt a sense of peace, inner calm, of fulfilment. I felt an escape, a freedom, a strange beauty that I hoped would last forever. "I reached back. I found His Lordship's hands as the tears began to flow. I relaxed back into him, his cock still deep inside me.

I have no idea how long we were like that, linked, united, by his cock.

He stood perfectly still when he did, eventually, pull out of me. I waited as long as I felt I could before moving.

I went to the locker and picked up a handtowel before finally turning to face him.

We looked each other directly in the eyes for the first time then. We didn't say anything, but there was a communication between us. I don't think to this day he was challenging me. I felt more as if he was inviting me to submit to him.

He was certainly an impressive man. I couldn't help but

wonder what he'd been like when he was twenty or thirty years younger. I tried to put such ideas out of my mind. I would never find his lost youth, nor would he, I thought.

I was in front of him before he pulled the condom off his cock. It wasn't fully hard, but it was still impressive. I hoped I'be be allowed to get to know it better. I was still looking down, wondering whether to wipe him myself or hand him the towel as he started to roll up the condom.

I sensed what to do as he brought the latex towards my lips.

I closed my eyes to relish the taste of his cum. He let a first drop fall on to my tongue. I let it linger, as much because of the significance of the action as the taste. A pleasant, salty aftertaste remained as he handed me the emptied condom. He took the towel and wiped himself as I put the condom into the trash and put the lube back into the locker.

'I need something to drink,' he said.

* * *

I left him, sitting close to Donaldson on the deck as I went to clean the dildo, put the towel and my shorts in the laundry. Donaldson had taken his cue from His Lordship in the barn. Luke was wearing no more than a tight pair of shorts as he brought His Lordship a large glass of freshly-squeezed orange juice.

The two men were talking when I followed Luke's instruction that I should go out to the deck.

A rug was on the wood, near His Lordship's chair. Donaldson nodded and I knelt down. I felt more comfortable just wearing a jock again, letting the warm late morning air brush against the nerve- endings in my freshly-shaved skin.

His Lordship leaned forward to rub my head as I knelt. I'd

done something right, I thought, perhaps a little too flippantly.

My interview started as soon as Donaldson went inside. There were, he'd said, some e-mails he needed to answers and some assignments to mark.

London-bound

That, said Andrew, was how it all began.

His Lordship asked about me, my background, my desires. I told him very much what I've told you, said Andrew. About Mary, the discovery which Donaldson had let happen, the lessons I'd learned from Luke.

His Lordship was friendly, loving even. He was apologetic about the intensity of the fuck. Had he, I'd asked, heard me complain, Andrew said.

'We had been talking for a while, when he sent me inside,' Andrew continued. 'I was to go and search for him online, to read what was there. I would learn more about him very quickly that he could tell me. Take your time, he'd instructed. Don't rush. He'd thought for a moment before looking up at me again. Did I, he'd asked, have a résumé? Or, better still, he said, a fuller CV? I had both. I'd been working on them with Luke. Donaldson had said that if I was to find a quality master, I had to have professional and life skills as well as sexual ones. I had to iron shirts, or organize a man's filing as well as I took a fucking or a beating, he'd said. Perhaps this was what was happening at this moment, I wondered, as I went to log on.

I took out my documents while the computer was booting.

'At least I'm in the right place to get very personal references,' His Lordship said as I knelt to hand him the papers. I had to smile. Yes, that was very true.

I found him engrossed in conversation with Donaldson when I went back out to the deck an hour or so later. He ignored me when I knelt down on the mat between them.

'I haven't had sex like that for longer than I can remember,' His Lordship said. 'I'm bi,' he added, looking at me. 'That had better not be a problem.'

I shook my head. From what I'd been able to find out from various news sites online, I didn't think there was anyone else in His Lordship's life. Whatever sex he'd been having had been very discrete.

'No, Sir, it isn't, Sir,' I said.

'Good. I like it hard. That's why Sarah left me. She said I was too violent, too dangerous. Perhaps it was the way I was raised? Eton and The Navy perhaps give you a false impression of masculinity. I like women, but Sarah thinks I'm too rough with them, that's why she wouldn't give me a divorce. She said it's her way of trying to protect other women from my ravages.

'That's not to say I don't like men, Donaldson. This man is very attractive, a fine specimen. He aroused many near-forgotten emotions and needs in me this morning.

'I don't know what I should call you,' he said, turning to me.

'My name has always been Andrew, Sir,' I said, 'but you can call me whatever you like.'

'I like people around me to have dignity,' he said, 'even when they're doing the most menial of work. You'll be Andrew to me then. Most of the time. Donaldson here says you're looking for a Master?'

'Sir, yes, I am, Sir,' I responded honestly.'

'What about me?'

I'd thought the question might be coming, but it's suddenness caught me off guard. Amos, Lord, Cunningham watched as I thought. I felt my answer, like the response to any command, should have been immediate.

'Don't worry, you can have time to think, Andrew. You'd be making quite a commitment, quite a life change. Donaldson tells me you'd like the way of life. Liking me would probably make the arrangement a lot easier – and enjoyable – for both of us.'

I had to agree with that. I still found it hard to submit to a man I didn't admire or respect. I liked Lord Cunningham's politics and his philosophies, at least as much of them as I'd been able to find out about online. I might not have been in Donaldson's circles long, but I'd already encountered Democrat slaves who found it impossible to kneel in front a dominant man who had even the lightest smell of being a Republican.

'Sir? A question, if I may, Sir, please?'

'Go ahead, Andrew, fire away.'

'What do you actually have in mind, Sir, please?'

'I was thinking I'd quite like to keep that ass of yours, Andrew. It made me so welcoming, and you control it so very, very well. But, as Donaldson here says, while that would be appropriate, it would also be failing to make use of some of your other talents and skills. I need some help with this inquiry. You'd be ideal for that. You understand the institutions, the agencies here better than I do. You probably know some of the personality politics too. If you don't, you know how to find out, who to ask, in ways that I don't.

'I've been given secretarial help of course,' he continued, 'but someone with broader abilities, and the experience to have an overview would be very valuable. Donaldson says you can do this, well. The staff I've been allocated are young. They're trying to make contacts for themselves, to network in search of their next career break. They don't have any loyalty, to me, or to the project. You would certainly have loyalty to me, and because of that, you'd be loyal to the project.

'I don't want to be rude, Andrew, but you and I, we're of an age now. We understand many of the ways of the world. We know when we have to be discrete, circumspect and we know when we can be more overt, more relaxed.

I was liking everything I heard.

'So, I'd be like a personal assistant, Sir?'

His Lordship grinned. 'Yes. A very personal assistant.'

'You'd be a fool not to, Andrew.' Donaldson was speaking now. I knew that, but I still didn't really know His Lordship, and my training in identifying, then avoiding, problems had tripped in. I was thinking logistically already.

'What about travel, Your Lordship? Health insurance?'

'Andrew's right, these need to be considered,' he replied, 'but I don't foresee any problems. If I tell my bosses in London, if I have a word with Cabinet Secretary, or the Prime Minister's chief of staff and say I need you, they'll arrange a diplomatic passport. You'll be able to cross the Atlantic whenever you need to. The bank will employ you, but we'll charge the UK government for your services. There'll be a management fee of course, but that will also cover all your health care, other insurances, and any costs incurred when you travel with me. Also, it will put our relationship entirely above board. You will appear with me in public, as my assistant, my inquiry manager. No one need know about your other, extracurricular activities.

I was starting to laugh.

'You've done this before, Sir,' I ventured.

'Some of it, not all, Andrew. Your salary would go into an account in case anything ever happened to me. You won't get a penny of it while I'm around. You'll be able to authorize payments on company accounts, but you'll be dependant on me for every penny in your pocket and accountable to me for it, I think that's only reasonable, don't you?'

I nodded. Lord Cunningham was really getting into this.

'Everything I think that you need will be paid for, whether it's what you eat, what you do, where you go, or what you wear. Is that clear?' I nodded again.

'You have manners. Donaldson has assured me of that, so I don't need to worry where I take you. And, with no public persona, at least at first, you can go shopping in places where my appearance may raise too many questions. Yes, the more I think about it, the more I like it,' he said.

Donaldson, as usual, came up with the compromise idea that made it all work.

'Your Lordship, Amos,' he said, you're not leaving here until Monday morning. It's still Saturday afternoon.'

I had to pinch myself, so much had happened, was happening, so quickly that day. 'Andrew can be yours for the weekend. If you're both happy, he can go with you on Monday.'

It still seemed something of a rush. Trying to fight it wouldn't work, I knew. Go with the flow, I told myself. Relax. See what happens.

'Luke is preparing dinner for eight,' said Donaldson. 'Why don't you go and have some time together? If you, or Amos, want anything from the leather closet, you never know, it may help, then feel free. Help yourselves.'

His Lordship was on his feet before I could speak.

'Come to my room in ten minutes,' he said to me. 'Donaldson, thank you.'

He shook Donaldson's hand enthusiastically before striding away.

'Go.' It was Donaldson's order. 'Get some water. Freshen up.'

I got up and made my way inside.

Luke hugged me as soon as I was in the kitchen.

'Listen,' he said, 'you've got it made like him. You couldn't be safer.'

I looked puzzled.

'It's obvious, dummy,' said Luke, putting his arm through mine, 'he's so prominent, publicly and politically, that if he fucks up, you can blow him out of the water.'

I must have looked uncomfortable.

'I wouldn't want to destroy his life,' I said.

'Of course,' said Luke. 'I know. It's not you. But remember, it's there. It's a safety net.'

I nodded, agreeing, reluctantly, but realistically.

'And, like the best safety nets, it should never be needed,' Luke added.

I was reassured then. Yes, I'd have some control, but it was an all-or-nothing way out. I'd probably destoy myself as well as his Lordship if I ever needed to use that way out. I hoped I'd never have to.

His Lordship was a different man for the next three hours. I spent time on my knees, gently sucking his immense cock as he sat back in a chair in his room. He let me strip him, then shower him, drying him down. He made me lie down on the bed, face up, my legs drawn up against my chest, while he fucked me again. Instead, of being brutal and wild, he was loving and gentle, moving so that he very, very gently rubbed my prostate until I was so high that I was clawing at the ceiling. I wondered what Sarah had been worried about out. "We raided Donaldson's leather closet before dinner. His Lordship was taller and thinner than Donaldson, but I managed to find some chaps, boots and a bar vest that made him look really good. I'd been thinking of wearing jeans, but His Lordship had other ideas when he saw a jockstrap.

He was happy when he came down to dinner. I'd gone downstairs ahead of him, so that I could help Luke with cocktails, but he had everything well under control. I needn't have worried.

After hearing His Lordship and me in the leather closet, Donaldson had dressed for dinner too. He'd chosen simply; nicely-cut leather pants and a Levi-like shirt and highly-polished boots. Luke was wearing a leather jockstrap, with bands around each of his upper arms. The pattern matched the studs on his collar.

I – or rather His Lordship – had chosen black leather shorts for me, the ones that just covered my butt. I would have felt better naked from the waist up, but His Lordship felt that a tanktop emphasized my shoulders. His wish, now, was my command. I found a design that was quite angular. When His Lordship suggested black, I suggested leather. No, he said, cotton would be fine.

He seemed to be happier when I used some initiative. While he wanted to be in command, in control, even in those few hours, I had gathered that he didn't want to micro-manage, unless he was really in the mood. I suspected that he was learning too.

His Lordship had, I sensed, always known what he wanted. Although he wasn't a born aristocrat, his upbringing – in the exclusive, expensive English boarding school, followed by university, his officer training in the Royal Navy – had reinforced his confidence and self- belief. Such establishments had long learned that – like the Ivy League establishments in the US and long-established schools of government and public administration in Europe – their purpose was to train those who would lead countries, businesses and the world's biggest and most influential organizations. Amos Cunningham was a proud product of such education.

I know that I responded to his self-assuredness. I'd always wondered about ego and individuals who reached such positions of influence, but His Lordship knew how to manage and present himself too. Even in such a short time, I had noticed that his arrogance could be turned on and off at will. He was a shrewd operator. There were occasions, I could see from the news reports I'd read online, that whatever he was really like, there were big occasions, or awkward negotiations when being arrogant to be point of being unreasonable had been the key factor that had, as far as His Lordship was concerned, won the day. Being arrogant, I imagined, added strength when others' interests were totally invested in one individual's determination and the poker-playing psychologies at play before someone blinked first. "I stood open-mouthed when His Lordship came into the dining room. He had found a plain black tee-shirt and a bar vest to with the black jockstrap and the chaps. The bare flesh displayed between his legs was so inviting. I found myself wanting to kneel and kiss him there.

His bare ass looked good too. His grin was almost child-like. He turned round as he approached Donaldson, showing off. 'What do you think?' Donaldson reached for his hands and kissed him. He looked astounded for a fraction of a second, then his laugh broke forth. He kissed Donaldson in return. He came and kissed me, then Luke.

'Hey, you guys,' said His Lordship, looking round, seeing surprise in our eyes, 'guys, isn't that what you say here in the colonies?'

He was teasing us all now.

'This is fun. I can't remember when I last had dinner with nothing covering my arse.'

He emphasized the different use of the word.

'When I was child, I suppose, when my nappy, my diaper,' he added, looking directly at Luke as the youngest man in the room, 'fell off. You guys really have learned how to wear some clothes and feel your bodies. Andrew, chaps; I shall want some.'

I nodded. I was looking forward to adding to His Lordship's wardrobe.

Donaldson hardly got to say a word over dinner. His Lordship was almost hyperactive. I thought, but I wasn't sure, that he was enjoying the fact that while Luke was serving Donaldson, I was serving him. Luke and I stood behind each man as they ate. We watched attentively, refilling their wine glasses, looking after their needs. We caught each others' eyes and smiled. We felt good doing what we were doing.

Luke had prepared food for us. We ate as we cleared the table and washed the dishes. Although Donaldson had a dishwasher, Luke insisted that all the glassware had to be washed and polished by hand. We took coffee and brandy out to Donaldson and His Lordship on the deck. This time, His Lordship was sitting forward, listening intently to what Donaldson was saying.

'Yes, yes,' were the only words I picked up as he concentrated on what Donaldson was saying. I noticed an innocence in him for the second time that evening. Whereas, before dinner, it had been his smiled that was youthful, now his eyes were childlike. I'd noticed the look before, in a baby, far too young to speak. The eyes looked as if they had been connected directly to the brain inside; the pleading being 'stimulate me, inform me, educate me'. I saw the same look in His Lordship's eyes. I knew then that he had never lost a passion for learning, for wanting to know more, know everything, whenever a subject or topic intrigued him.

'There is,' Donaldson was saying as Luke and I made our way back out to the deck, 'a finesse to what we do. People mistakenly think that SM is violent. It may be intense, yes, but it is not violent.'

His Lordship looked puzzled.

Donaldson noticed. 'Let me explain,' he said. 'I think violence occurs when someone doesn't consent. In SM, the bottom, the boy, the slave, call the person what you will, has consented. However heavy the activity may be, whatever apparent damage has been caused, it should be use, not abuse,' Donaldson stressed. 'Break the skin, yes, but don't break bones. Don't put someone in the hospital. Don't damage their mind either.'

Donaldson was on a roll now.

'That's often more difficult,' he said, 'because none of us ever knows, really, what a chance, off-hand remark could trigger. That's why a good Master has to know a slave's mind as well as the slave. Ideally, he should know that mind better. I don't want a slave that's like an unruly child, a spoiled brat who has become conditioned by the perception that the only way to get attention is to be disruptive, to have temper tantrums and hissy fits. Like many, I will not tolerate a slave that intentionally fucks up in order to create a scene or provoke a confrontation.'

His Lordship was paying close attention, taking in every word. I smiled as, almost without realizing it, he reached out and rubbed my head when I sat down, cross-legged beside his chair.

'Yes,' Donaldson went on, 'slaves may need to be punished. That is a crucial part of this way of life. We shouldn't use emotional blackmail. We shouldn't over act being hurt or disappointed. By bringing the authority into the open, we can say something is wrong, there and then, and deal with it.'

His Lordship nodded.

'Yes,' he said, 'that makes a lot of sense.'

'The difficulty,' said Donaldson, 'is in knowing what makes a punishment effective. We have to re-assess many aspects of our own early conditioning. We have to examine what we mean by pain, for example.'

He stopped for a moment, thinking about where his discourse was going.

'It's why I like working in academe, Amos. I have access to the greatest minds and the greatest collected knowledge and wisdom. Some of my colleagues probably wouldn't appreciate knowing the context of my curiousity. Others have been fascinated.

'I've learned about pain, the nervous system and how we learn to interpret the stimuli of impact or of intense heat as signals telling us that unless we move, our bodies are likely to be damaged. We can unlearn some of that on our own. We can see how long we can hold our fingers near a flame before we flinch, for example. Then, there are the extra dimensions that come from doing this with another person. There can be the immeasurable intensity that comes from trusting another person with such delicate judgments about damage, in letting them decide where that infinitesimally thin line lies on the cusp between ecstasy and the agony of damage. There can be the endorphin, drug-like, high as the nervous system reacts to the stimulation.

'This is maelstrom of paradox, Amos. If you want to punish someone through pain, by making something hurt, can you then use paddle as a deterrent on a man who has learned to enjoy the stimulation that the impact of wood on bare ass produces?'

Donaldson paused.

'Personally, I don't think so. That pain is about context is a key aspect of what this is all about. We have to think, be imaginative about what we do. If a slave wants to give me control of his sexual release, then telling him that he is not allowed to touch his cock, or even locking it up, is ineffective. I have to find yet another way of punishment. Deprivation, Amos, is probably most straightforward. If you want to punish, deprive a slave of what he wants most. If that's your cock, then so be it, you have to make a sacrifice too.

'You and I may see a cage as representing the loss of liberty. For a slave, the bars may epitomize protection, keeping all the threats and dangers of the world at bay. We may feel trapped. He may feel safe, secure. He could be retreating to the fetal. We would be manic,' he said.

His Lordship relaxed a little then; he sat back in his chair.

'Yes,' I see what you mean,' he said, looking at Donaldson. 'If I look to different contexts – business, the military – I can find parallels.'

He looked down at me, grinning, rubbing his hand over my forearm where it rested on his thigh.

'Andrew will help,' said Donaldson. 'He's had to learn a lot about himself too, and very quickly. He knows what books to recommend. He knows people whom you might appreciate meeting. He has, I hope, learned who to avoid, some of the characters in a very small world, who have not developed the discretion that a hostile world demands of us.

'There are books here, but,' Donaldson paused, shaking his head, 'you don't really have enough time. Andrew can get the ones you really should read.'

Although only a few hours had passed, Donaldson seemed entirely convinced that I'd be leaving with His Lordship on the Monday morning. I didn't know what His Lordship did feel, but almost by proxy, Donaldson had already appointed me to his side.

I knew that my feelings for him were deepening. Just being so close to him was making me feel valued and wanted, desires that, I had come to realize, were vitally important to me. Underneath the business suits, there was a sexy man with a huge cock, big balls and a butt that had not succumbed to the gravity of age. I felt my own cock starting to fill as I looked lovingly at His Lordship's jockstrap, framed by the naked skin between the leather legs of the chaps.

I pulled myself on to my knees and turned, pulling my face between His Lordship's knees. I could feel him smile as he rubbed my head. I sensed Donaldson grinning too; I'd learned what gave him pleasure, directly and indirectly, during my time at his home.

His Lordship kept my head between his leathered thighs as he picked up his brandy goblet, cupping the glass with both hands. I heard him swirl the Cognac. I glanced upwards to see him hold the goblet beneath his nose so he could inhale and savor the spirits rising from the amber liquid. Only then did he release a few drops on to his tongue. I imagined the initial perception of burning before the flavors ran to the mouth's different tastebuds.

My elbows were on His Lordship's knees, my arms along his thighs, my hands parallel with his jockstrap. I very gently squeezed him. Without words, I wanted to tell him that I understood his appreciation of quality.

I hadn't expected him to bend forward and kiss my forehead. I could smell the brandy on his lips. He put a finger into the glass, capturing a droplet. He placed it on my lips. As carefully as I could, I pushed my tongue forward, not wanting to dislodge the moisture. I was picking up the aroma of perspiration between his legs. The combination of the two was beyond words.

I succumbed, gently letting my mouth forward as His Lordship increased the pressure on the back of my head, taking my time from his. I kissed the jockstrap as my lips met that point where the base of his cock met the ball sac. Despite my concentration, I could sense activity behind me too. Luke, I guessed, was also putting his mouth to good use in pleasuring Donaldson.

I was licking the jockstrap more when I heard Luke moving. I kept my eyes closed as he went down the wooden steps. A few moments later, the sound of the barn door opening reached my ears. I kept licking, running my tongue up and down His Lordship's trapped cock, or nibbling on the cloth-covered balls, as I listened. I pushed his legs apart with my head so that I could lick the sweat from his perineum. I tried to get to his hole, but could only just reach it with the tip of my tongue. I was sure that I heard a first groan of pleasure as I did. I knew my efforts were appreciated when he squeezed my hand.

'Um, nice,' I heard Donaldson say as Luke returned. I heard some clatter, the sound of chains, metal studs, were put down on a table. "His Lordship didn't seem to object as Donaldson and Luke added to my stimulation. I kept my mouth on the pouch of the jockstrap as His Lordship stood up. I pulled the jock over his cock and balls with my mouth, pulling the waistband down at the sides as far as the chaps would allow.

I was sucking on His Lordship's balls when Luke attached the first of the clamps to my nipples. I turned my chest so he could attach the second. I kept my mouth full as he pulled my butt up from the kneeling position. His Lordship chuckled as Luke pulled the tight shorts down my legs. I lifted one booted foot at a time so he could lift them out of the way.

I spread my legs obediently so that Luke could my balls back between my legs and screw the humbler device into place. My cock was hard as I felt the wood come to rest against the back of my thighs.

I was trying to take as much of His Lordship's mighty member down my throat as I could when I felt fingers against my hole. Instinctively, I spread my legs to try to allow easier access. His Lordship reached down and played with my nipples as lube was eased into my hole. I still felt used, if not exactly sore, from His Lordship's bestial fuck earlier in the day, but I tried to ignore any discomfort in favor of remembering its intensity as a plug was eased into me.

I moaned as the fingers added to the pressure of the nipple clamps. I bucked a little as pressure against the plug in my ass increased and the tip hit my prostate.

Opening my mouth as the first stroke of the cane hit my butt got me into the position where His Lordship's cock went further into my throat. I thought I was gagging, but whoever was beating me was watching carefully, letting me breath through my nose between strokes.

I think I must have taken at least six when the cock was suddenly pulled from my mouth.

I desperately wanted to see what was happening, but somehow I kept my eyes closed. I sense His Lordship moving away from me. Another man was in front of me; Luke. I felt his hands on my shoulders as I braced myself, my hands on my slightly bent knees.

I felt his jockstrap against my face. I sensed him bend forward.

'Lick if it helps,' he whispered into my ear.

The plug was pressed again.

'Nice,' said His Lordship.

My mind was racing. I felt a hand between my legs, feeling for my erection.

'Even nicer,' he said as his hand gripped my cock and started squeezing. I tried to open my legs further, pushing my pelvis back, so that he could do what he wanted. I hoped he would sense what I was trying to do.

I wasn't sure why, but I'd been expecting the next impact to come from another stroke of the cane. I jumped a little in surprise as a paddle came down against my balls. I heard the sound of a chair as someone, His Lordship, sat down.

I could sense Donaldson as conductor, directing His Lordship as the percussion against my trapped sac continued. The implements would change, from something smooth and flat, to something rougher and rounder. The tempo would increase, decrease; the intensity would increase, decrease. Donaldson was tutoring a willing pupil. His Lordship would alternate the rapid and gentle with less frequent but harder blows. I could feel the soreness starting in my balls.

Luke kept up his gentle rocking of my shoulders throughout. The pouch of his jockstrap was almost saturated, I'd been drooling so much throughout the drumming on my scrotum.

I felt his grip increase when the ball beating stopped. This, I sensed, was when the caning would begin again.

'How many?' asked His Lordship.

'He took eight before,' answered Donaldson. 'He can take more.'

'At school,' said His Lordship, 'they were always

administered in sixes. Let's see how he does with a first half-dozen.'

I felt Luke supporting me as I braced myself. I knew Donaldson's style, how hard he would hit. I had no idea of what His Lordship would, or could do.

I sensed him pause. I heard the swish as he moved the cane through the air.

'I haven't done this for decades,' he said. 'It brings back memories.'

Someone must have looked puzzled.

'At school, the prefects were allowed to cane the boys, for minor misdemeanors.'

He was sniggering.

'Some of us were real sadists,' he said. 'We probably beat them far harder than the schoolmasters ever did.'

I was taken aback when I felt His Lordship kneel down beside me. I felt his face in mine. I felt the cane against my lips. I kissed it.

'That's right, Andrew,' he whispered. 'Make me happy.'

I nodded, just.

'Yes, Sir.'

I could feel his breath, deep and warm, against my cheek.

'Open your eyes,' he ordered. 'Look down.'

I did. The huge cock was pointing up at me, a droplet of pre-cum forming at the piss-slit. I wanted to kiss it, to lick up that bead of honey.

'Are you ready?' He held my hand as he looked into my eyes.

'Yes, Sir,' I said as the first tears started to ooze from their ducts. 'I'm ready, Sir.'

I closed my eyes again as His Lordship stood. Luke returned to his place in front of me, replacing his hands on my shoulders. I rested my lips against his pouch.

I felt another hand on me, on my back, my shoulder blade. I glanced quickly. It was Donaldson, adding his support.

'Six it will be, Andrew,' said His Lordship.

I nodded very deliberately, hoping that he had seen the acknowledgement.

Wow; they came hard and fast. I'd hardly opened my mouth after the first impact before they were over. My ass was aflame. My tongue was pressing against Luke. I was panting. My throat was suddenly dry. I couldn't have screamed, however much I wanted to. I was trying to control my breathing as the plug was pulled from my hole.

'Yes!' I gasped again as His Lordship's cock forced its way into me I felt his flesh against the burning skin of my ass, the heat glowing as the welts from the caning were most intense. I screamed silently against Luke as his thrusts again hit my prostate. The tears ran from my eyes, dripping from my cheeks to the deck below me.

Capitulation

The stripes were beautifully defined when I looked at them in the mirror the next morning.

My ass still hurt, but I was proud of my performance. My hole was sore from the second brutal fucking, my nipples sensitive from the clamps.

His Lordship had lost none of his teenage skills with a cane, I thought, as I took his coffee up the stairs. He had lost none of his virility either, fucking me three times within less than twelve hours.

His libido was still hungry when I put the coffee down in the room.

'Come here,' he said, lifting the comforter so I could get into the bed beside him.

'Suck,' he ordered, pushing my head down onto his aggressive morning erection.

I hadn't been between his legs for very long when I heard the condom being unwrapped.

'Turn over,' he said.

I did as I was told.

I put my face into one of the pillows as His Lordship very gently started to lube my hole. I was pleased I'd had a quick douche over the bidet when I got up, and rubbed some balm into the membrane around my violated sphincter.

'Open up for me, Andrew,' he whispered as he pushed my legs apart and raised my butt, placing my hole against his hard cock.

For the second time, he entered me very tenderly. Again, he positioned himself so that he could rub his cock against my prostate. I could feel his cock head teasing my inner ring as he pushed his pelvis against me. He was big and he could get right in. What more, I thought facetiously, could a pig want?

I could feel my own cock starting to drip, as the prostate stimulation continued. I'd been milked by a man using his hand once. This, I thought was much more beautiful.

I closed my eyes as His Lordship started to increase the frequency and intensity of his thrusts. I tried to co-ordinate my breathing with his.

I felt the muscles in his legs tense as his orgasm approached.

I felt mine tensing too.

'Yes!'

His fingernails were digging into my upper arms as he shot. He was panting against the back of my neck.

Without realizing it, I was shooting too. I fucked myself with his cock, using the head to force the cum out from my prostate.

I was panting too, but it still took His Lordship a few moments to notice what had happened.

'You shouldn't have done that, Andrew,' he said. 'You didn't have permission.'

I turned round and kissed him on the lips.

'Yes, Sir. I know, Sir. You may have to punish me, Sir, I said.

He kissed me then, passionately, forcefully, pushing his tongue into my mouth.

'I might have to reward you instead,' he said. 'Or make it a rule that that's the only way you ever get to cum; no touching, only me inside you.'

I reached for his hands and squeezed them.

I pulled my mouth away from his just long enough to say 'I consent to that, Sir.'

* * *

And yes, Andrew told me, of course I left with him on the Monday. He'd made some calls that Sunday afternoon. I don't know who he called, or what he said. I can guess, but I was expected when we arrived in New York on the Monday afternoon. I think both his assistants were pissed to get such calls when they were making the most of their weekends.

I was sent out, to buy new business suits and shoes, while His Lordship took some meetings. I flew back to the UK with him a few days later. Sitting beside him in first class, I remembered one of the stories I'd read. I wasn't the first slave to travel in luxury.

The Cunningham Report was a killer.

He presented it with the panache that was expected. He pleased everyone; I don't know how he did it to this day. The UK government was pleased. The universities were pleased. The industry was delighted. The media acclaim verged on the histrionic.

He was a star again. We were feted wherever we went. No one questioned our relationship. I carried his bags, or arranged for them to be carried. I made his calls, planned the schedules, I moved into his London home.

I arranged the conversion of his Belgravia basement from a storage room into a playroom and a gym. I bought leather and equipment from the world's best manufacturers.

During the day, I'd be quietly calm. I was going to say that since I've been with him, I've probably worked harder than at any time in my life, but it doesn't feel like work; it feels like having a full life.

I can't remember when I last touched my cock. It's usually locked away. I don't really need it. I have the beautiful monster between his legs to keep me satisfied now.

His Lordship still works. Since the report, he can charge thousands per hour for advising big pharma. He arranged share options in the bank for me too. They don't know it, but Annie and George, my kids, they'll be worth a lot too, in time.

He has relaxed too, enough to come to a few events such as this. Of course, we're still careful. Some gatherings are too open, but this, two hundred and fifty guys who can afford to be here, it's OK. Sure, it may be expensive, too expensive for some good, enthusiastic guys who could contribute or learn a lot, but that, I think, is a price worth paying.

Andrew reached for my hand then.

'That, I think,' he said, 'brings you about up-to-date.'

I nodded. I thought it did.

I said nothing as Andrew added more polish to one of His Lordship's boots.

'When are you going back?' he asked me a few moments later.

'Friday,' I said.

'And in London next?'

'Thursday next week. I have a meeting.'

* * *

Dinner that evening was another pleasurable experience. I don't know what Andrew had said, but it was clear from the outset that I should kneel beside him, rather than use the table. I'd appreciated that.

I hadn't had too much more time with either His Lordship or Andrew during the rest of the run.

We were about to leave when Andrew came up to me. He gave me a business card, one of His Lordship's.

'If you have a meeting on Thursday, you can be in London on Wednesday afternoon,' he said. 'Six o'clock sharp. I think you know what to do.'

THE END

About the Author

Chris Charlton is in his fifties and has been interested in power relationships and SM for more than thirty five years. He is a professional writer and journalist, covering health, including HIV, and the media. He takes his play and relationships seriously, being a long-standing member of one pf the leading SM clubs in the US. He read psychology at university in England.

Taking inspiration from leading writers such as John Preston, Race Bannon, Joseph Bean, 'Fledermaus' and Guy Baldwin, Chris Charlton looks for the beautiful, the positive and the inspirational in the honesty that allows people to appreciate the power dynamics of dominance and willing submission.

Chris's interests include many aspects of physical SM, the exploration of the body and its responses. He is also intrigued by the ways in which finding and being open about the power dynamics between people can keep the most intimate relationships alive and exciting.

Retirement is the final part of a trilogy first in a series of stories exploring domestic power relationships and the minds of those attracted to them.

You can write to Chris at chrschrltn@gmail.com